Queeird

A Collection of Unusual
Trans Masculine Erotica

Max Turner

Contents

Creature Features & Furries

The Inevitable Tentacles

About the Author

AuthoꞱ's Note

This collection is the result of not enough submission calls for publications that take a combination of trans stories, erotica, and monster fuckery!

The stories herein range in genre, style, and length. Some are less taboo than others, some are more character-led, but all are sex-positive and erotic. In some, the character's transness is integral to the story; in others, it is incidental.

All the stories feature trans masculine characters with a variety of lovers including cis, trans and non-binary.

It may be the case that these stories aren't for everyone, but I hope you find at least one that you love. This is the risk with picking up any collection or anthology, but I acknowledge for trans readers especially, it may come down to the language used and the specifics of the stories. It is therefore for the comfort of my trans, non-binary, genderqueer, and otherwise non-cis readers, that I have included a list of content warnings at the start of each story, and an indication of the sort of language used to describe trans anatomy. Most include PIV (penis in vagina) penetration, and the terminology used is a mixture of masculine and feminine. Heed the warnings and enjoy!

HaLLUCiNOgeNS

&

HeXeS

L^e^da

Sam and Sebastian explore a new kink.

Content Notes: Trans man/cis Man.
BDSM, sub/Dom, pain-play, spanking, wax-play,
sex toys, consensual non-consent, consensual
somnophilia, breeding kink, impregnation kink,
sedation, drug use (psilocybin mushroom),
hallucinations, giant man-swan thing.
Anatomical references: PIV penetration, mention
of past hysterectomy. G-spot and pussy used for
trans male genitalia.

"I am so pleased to be able to bring you here
finally." Sebastian's voice was low, and he
practically purred the words against Sam's ear as
they walked from the car to Sebastian's Hamptons
home.

It was modest, as far as a house in the
Hampton's could be, but it echoed the same sleek
mid-century aesthetic of Sebastian's New York City
home. It was easy to admire the beautiful setting as
Sebastian let them in and closed the door softly
behind them. But, as beautiful as it was, they
weren't there to enjoy their surroundings, at least
not in that respect.

They had been meeting at the club since they hooked up there that first night. And while there had also been dates, even overnights, neither did this in their New York homes. Now, it was time to explore things more privately to see if they could be fully compatible in both a romantic and a sub/Dom relationship.

Given Sam's penchant for pain without submission, it had never really been a typical sub/Dom relationship, but they provided for each other what they needed and enjoyed. With their romantic relationship deepening, they both felt it was time to integrate the two aspects of their lives more seamlessly, and what better place to do that than the playroom in Sebastian's Hampton's home?

There was an added benefit of this feeling of being removed from the everyday. It gave them space to explore and push boundaries, separate from the rest of their lives in a setting more private than a club.

Even as Sebastian showed him around, Sam was growing wet in anticipation of what would come.

Sebastian saved the playroom for last, showing Sam the main living areas, the bedroom, and the bathrooms. It was a modest size considering Sebastian's NYC penthouse, and Sam wondered if the entire purpose was just somewhere to have a playroom. Especially once he saw it, much more well-equipped than most clubs he'd frequented.

The fact that the house was relatively isolated, and the windows looked soundproofed sent a thrilled tingle up Sam's spine.

He remained in a state of agitated interest whilst

they prepared and ate a light dinner and drank some wine as evening descended. And he knew Sebastian was aware of this – drawing out the inevitable encounter. While Sam would have been happy to head immediately to the playroom on their arrival, Sebastian would want to tease Sam a little. He was just as keen to play but also savoured the light torture this caused for Sam. He couldn't imagine Sebastian had missed that he'd been in various states of arousal since the car pulled up outside.

As they shared heated glances across the dinner table, there was no denying this was foreplay for them both.

Sam moaned as he felt the rope bite into his skin as it was tightened, leaning into the rack that tilted him at an angle and left him looking at the floor.

It had been a long time since they last did this. In part because it held a certain kind of intimacy for them. A rack like this at the club had been the first thing they had experienced together and back then, as Sebastian had selected a crop, he'd muttered soft words.

"I want to strap you to a rack, give you the pain you crave and fuck you as hard as you wish, rough if you prefer. And then I will tend to your wounds, bathe you if you'd let me, take you to my bed, and when you're rested, I would like to make love with you."

Just remembering his words all these months later made Sam shiver. From that moment, their connection had been undeniable, not just another play session with another clubgoer.

He wasn't expecting lovemaking this time. No, this was pure play. But that didn't stop his dick from throbbing at the memory of that first night together after the club.

Sam had been looking forward to this all week. Not just the pain but to be at Sebastian's mercy again. It had been hard to give it up before, even knowing he could take it back whenever he asked. Sebastian had been the only person Sam had wholly submitted to –when he felt like it.

The week of anticipation had been painful in itself.

"Master Rockford...." The name issued as a whine as Sebastian pulled the ropes tightly to secure them. It was a perfect, pained stretch. "Fuck me..." he growled.

Sebastian chuckled at Sam's breathless demand and spanked a flat, hard palm across his ass, to which Sam rocked into the rack, causing another whine of delighted and agonised frustration.

"Not in a position to give orders, are we, Mr Jackson? Perhaps it's been too long since we did this. Perhaps you've forgotten your manners?"

Sam panted a laugh, sweat sticking his hair to his forehead and dripping down into his eyes.

"Maybe your previous lessons haven't been as effective as you'd hoped, *Master*." Sam taunted and received another sharp slap for his insolence.

He loved this. *God,* he loved this!

He loved the way Sebastian put up with his shit. He'd played with other Doms before but never in the long term, and this was part of the reason. Sam was a challenging sub. It could be argued he wasn't a sub at all. He wanted the pain, and he was willing to submit for it, but he was far from submissive. In the long term, many Doms weren't on board with that. It wasn't what they wanted out of a mutually satisfying arrangement. They wanted a submissive, and even those who didn't mind meting out the pain for minor infringements didn't want someone who would constantly backchat them and only submit on their own terms.

Sebastian, however, loved it. It suited him.

He'd made it very clear to Sam, over and over, both in words and actions, that Sam being contrary didn't bother him in the least. He liked the playfulness of being able to punish Sam for it, and he did love handing out a good spanking. But as great a Dom as Sebastian was, he wasn't in it to dominate in the same way many Sam had played with in the past.

Sure, he liked inflicting the pain, but it was clearly always because he knew Sam enjoyed receiving it. More than that – that Sam wanted and *needed* it. Sebastian just wanted to give subs what they needed from him, a service top at heart. And Sam had a feeling that had never been truer than with himself.

In and out of the playroom, Sebastian wanted to give Sam everything.

And it was, surprisingly, not as suffocating as Sam had imagined it might be. It made what they were developing possible.

He gasped in pain as the rack shifted, pulling

him taut. They hadn't used one in a while, so Sebastian wasn't going to really stretch him tonight, Sam knew. But the burn of even this little bit was enough to keep Sam hard and wet.

"Master," Sam sighed, an edge of pain there, and Sebastian let out a responding hum of approval. Always so haughtily formal in these situations, it sometimes felt like the most perverse thing about it.

"Are you enjoying this, Mr Jackson? It's been too long since I had you at my mercy like this."

Sam released a shuddering breath. Face down, he had no idea what Sebastian was doing but could hear him moving around. Preparing.

They had discussed many times at length what their limits were, and Sam had readily agreed that as long as nothing was introduced *beyond* his limits, he would happily take what Sebastian would give him without prior warning.

A crop? A flogger? Maybe he would simply continue to spank him for a while first?

Sam's breath hitched, and a cry broke from his throat as he felt the heat. His arousal waned slightly for a few moments as his mind adjusted to what his body was feeling – the hot wax dripped over his back. It would be little more than a flash of heat from a greater height – just a hint of what pain it could bring. But Sebastian moved it as close as he could without causing real damage. Close enough that Sam groaned with the burn, knowing it would leave sensitive, red patches across his back, his ass, his thighs.

"You are exquisite when you're in pain, breathtaking," Sebastian muttered. He leaned in close, his words a hot breath against Sam's ear, "How delightfully pleasing you will be when I flog over these lovely marks."

Sam sobbed and tried not to come.

"Sam, how do you feel about somnophilia?" Sebastian dropped the question into the dinner conversation as though they were discussing the weather.

Far from being shocked by anything Sebastian might say or do at this point, Sam's first reaction was to grin and then let out a soft chuckle as Sebastian's face creased in concentration while he carefully carved the meat joint.

Sam raised a brow and adjusted himself in the chair, his ass and back still smarting in the most wonderful way from the evening before.

"I'm... not opposed. Not something I'd much thought about before," Sam responded, taking a sip of his wine whilst intently and intensely watching Sebastian over the rim. "Whom did you envisage would be the slumbering party in this tryst?"

"That, I had pictured as you, but if you'd prefer—"

"No, no, I'm more than willing to... explore." Sam took another sip and gave a nod of thanks as Sebastian placed the food in front of him. "Can I ask what your *interest* is in this? Is it the thought of a slumbering, near lifeless body, or the idea of a lack of consent?"

Sebastian licked his lips then sucked his lower

lip between his teeth, holding it there momentarily before releasing it as he considered Sam's question, "The latter."

Sam cocked a questioning brow, admittedly surprised by the response, which Sebastian observed with a slight twitch of a smile on his lips. He had never before expressed an interest in any non-con play.

"I suppose, as we are here and ensuring our compatibility, I want to reveal the furthest extent of my desires and see if you are comfortable with that."

Sam nodded, "this would seem to be the time and the place. What is it you have in mind?"

"It is... rather more involved, if you'll indulge me?"

"By all means," Sam allowed, setting his wine down and giving Sebastian his full attention.

"A while ago, I came into possession of a rather beautiful toy that I have not yet had the chance to make use of. At the time, I acquired it because it pleased me aesthetically. Still, it was some time before I realised the connection to other pieces of art in my possession." He paused for a moment and tilted his head in question, "Are you familiar with the myth of Leda and the Swan?"

Sam shook his head and replied, "Vaguely, it's a Greek Myth."

"Quite so, it is the myth of a mortal woman seduced by Zeus whilst he is in the form of a swan."

"Kinky in itself," Sam mused with an indulgent smile that Sebastian returned.

"And in this scenario, you wish for me to play

the part of Leda, and you the swan, or more accurately, the *King* of the Gods." Sam clarified with a tease, intrigued as to what the toy could be that would transform Sebastian in such a way.

"Yes, I'm not wishing to stick strictly to the myth, but to a fantasy of my own, if you'd be willing...." Sebastian's hesitation was manufactured and he continued, "She bore Zeus's children whilst at the same time bearing her husband's children. So later myths would have it. I, of course, would not expect you to beget my young."

"I'm relieved to hear it," Sam took another sip of wine, grinning against the glass. Discussions on a vast number of topics with Sebastian were often amusing and entertaining, and this was far from an exception. "I'm still unsure how I feel about oviposition, so that option is off the table for now."

They had discussed all topics of impregnation and gestation when their romantic relationship became serious. Sam's hysterectomy had been years before, and he had no desire for children, which Sebastian shared. But he was certainly intrigued by the idea of a breeding kink and decided he might quite enjoy it.

Sebastian could barely hide his smile – Sam always enjoyed it when that happened – and then slowly inclined his head in agreement. Of course, the man had considered that as part of this scenario, and *of course*, Sam had known that would be the case. He wondered whether Sebastian already had some eggs stored away, awaiting this conversation.

Sam's lips picked up into a smile. There was

something quite beguiling about Sebastian wanting to enact a specific fantasy of his own. He had never shared anything quite as personal before, and it undoubtedly gave Sebastian a strange kind of vulnerability, considering Sam would be the one getting ravaged.

"You think I need to be asleep for you to truly dominate me," Sam wondered aloud.

Sebastian hesitated in picking up his glass as though he genuinely hadn't considered that, but now very much was.

"Sometimes you know my mind better than I do," he admitted, "I believe there may be an element of that."

Sam scoffed into his wine, which Sebastian chose to ignore.

"Leda wasn't sleeping," Sam ventured, "but you want me to be. The full consensual, non-consensual works."

"As I said, my fantasy differs a little from the myth. One could argue that the way Zeus seduced was non-consensual. He had a power over these women that made them compliant. They might as well have been sleeping."

"Ah! You're not confident that you could bewitch me?" Sam challenged good-naturedly.

Sebastian raised a brow, "I'm more concerned that the tables would be turned. I've never made a secret of the power you hold over me, Sam."

Sam blushed and raised his glass to drink, hiding his reddening face and stalling.

"I propose a light sedation, perhaps some psilocybin mushroom if you'd be willing? And of course, you would be prepared thoroughly first. My hope is that you will wake during—"

"And be so besotted with my God King that I would, in effect, have been seduced."

Sebastian's jaw tightened, and Sam wondered if he was getting hard. It was tempting to toe off a shoe under the table and seek evidence in Sebastian's lap.

"Sedation, preparation, then you will seduce me as a swan, and I will wake, passionately willing to bear your young."

Sebastian let out a shuddering breath, his eyes dark.

"The mushrooms… I don't like being in an altered state." Sam reminded Sebastian of something he was sure to be aware of already. Subspace was one thing, but not being in control to such an extent was something he didn't like.

Sebastian inclined his head slightly, "I anticipated only a small amount if you trust—"

"Would you like it, Sebastian? You do so much for me, give me the pain I crave… I *need*. The least I can do is indulge your fantasy." Sam set down his wine and used the napkin to dab at his lips before rising. He walked around the table until he stood next to Sebastian, offering a hand for him to take.

"You owe me nothing. This scene only happens if you want it."

Sam smiled, "Seduce me, my God King."

Sam woke with a motion.

A sway.

A gentle but firm press that had his hips rocking into the bed beneath him.

Knowing what was happening came to him slowly and made him moan, his cock instantly throbbing at both the thought and the friction. He'd honestly had no idea he would find it so immediately arousing. But the thought of Sebastian having waited for him to sleep and then eased himself inside, taking advantage of his prone body as they had agreed, made him shiver.

It took him a moment, the almost entire pulling out, the pause before pushing back in – to realise that it wasn't Sebastian inside him.

He felt a moment of panic then, wondering how terribly this could have gone wrong. How he had, and would never make himself vulnerable like this for anyone other than Sebastian. Sebastian, who he trusted entirely, who he…

The push back in was cool enough to make him shiver again but at the physical sensation this time.

The toy, it was a toy.

Whatever it was, it was the thing that had inspired Sebastian's fantasy.

The sedation had left him heavy; everything blurred and askew from the mushrooms. His limbs were like lead, and movement didn't come readily. This sensation wasn't appealing, and Sam whimpered, squirming slightly, tensing.

Resistance had him clenching around the toy.

"Shhh," Sebastian's voice soothed, and he felt a feather-light touch against his thigh. A soft that wasn't entirely Sebastian's. He was wearing soft, light gloves, and they felt both alien and wonderful against Sam's skin. "Let me have you, my darling Leda."

Sam wanted to look but couldn't quite lift his head enough, the attempt making his mind swim. Instead, he was left picturing the scene from what he could feel. From what he could imagine.

Sebastian was a great swan, his wings beating as he positioned himself between Sam's legs and sheathed himself within him.

Sam groaned at the push, his arousal mounting once more as his foggy mind alternated between Sebastian and a swan, not brilliant white, but black with hungry red eyes.

Sebastian was gentle, as he was when they made love, not rough as it often was when they played together.

Sam realised that was what this was, how Sebastian viewed it. But then, he had started to understand over time that even in their scenes, even when he was inflicting pain upon Sam's willing flesh, Sebastian was making love.

He groaned again, feeling his cock throbbing with his want. The sheets beneath him felt rough compared to Sebastian's soft touch, feathers exploding in Sam's mind.

"Want to see you…" Sam managed to expel the words with a little effort. His mind was swimming, and his grasp of reality fluctuated, making him feel nauseous.

Sebastian withdrew, and Sam sobbed at the loss even though he'd anticipated it.

Gentle hands moved over him then, one lifting

him to slide another pillow behind him, raising him so he could make out a looming figure in the darkness.

He was a man, but Sam's mushroom-addled imagination provided more from the shadows across the room. Great wings sprouted from his back, black feathers across broad swaths of his pale skin, and his hands were black, all the way up to his elbows.

His eyes, red. Burning red.

Sam couldn't entirely focus on him, or perhaps Sebastian wasn't wholly there.

Maybe it was Zeus?

Hands glided over his skin, up and down his flanks, tender motions as he was positioned, and gentle hands spread his legs wide.

The swan filled his vision, covering the entire room, shadows and all. Sebastian's dark feathers expanded into every space as he loomed large above him.

The Sebastian-swan didn't move forward, didn't thrust into him, but his presence felt oppressive all the same, and Sam wondered if it was a trick of the light. Maybe there was nothing there at all.

No, black hands were moving, barely visible between his legs. Perhaps the swan's penis was so large it needed to be guided in such a way?

Sam's head swam, and it thumped back onto the pillows, no longer able to hold himself up enough to watch. Not just from the hazy fog he found himself in but from pleasure as the swan glided into him. He couldn't quite feel the touch of it against his g-spot, but his body registered the pleasure of it.

The sensation was bizarre, slightly numb all over; he began to moan at the motion, at the thrusts. His hips were lifting to meet the swan, and the whole room seemed engulfed in feathers.

"Deeper, deeper…" Sam begged, a slurred edge to his words as he sank into the fantasy, "Sire your children…."

"Leda…" Sebastian's voice was rough.

Sam whined as he felt him pull away, felt the swan pull out of his body, leaving him empty.

He was about to protest, but then smooth hands held him down, gripped against his arms. Then Sebastian was leaning over him, keeping his legs spread with the weight of his body as he slid into him.

And this was different.

Whereas before, the swan had been cool and rigid, now he was filled with a firm warmth. With Sebastian.

Sam's breath caught as the Sebastian-swan began to fuck into him, rough and deep. Pushing against him to fold him increasingly over, increasingly deeper until Sam couldn't speak. He couldn't do anything but lie there and take it.

He grew wetter at the thought. Not something he might ever have considered arousing, nor something he would have thought Sebastian would be aroused by; they both were strongly reacting to this situation.

And he knew, even in his half-fuzzed brain, he knew that it wasn't wholly the idea of this being non-consensual, even though it was a facsimile of it. It was the thought of Sam's submissiveness that aroused Sebastian not just in this way but that he'd submitted to the entire scenario.

And Sam loved it, especially as the tingle of feeling returned to his body and Sebastian thrust harder and deeper to the point of pain.

"My King!" He cried out just before Sebastian's mouth covered his own, and his body pressed him into the mattress so hard that Sam could feel the cutting edge of sharp feathers. Could feel the dark wings enveloping him as Sebastian spilled inside his fertile body.

Sam awoke sore.

Everything hurt. As though his body had been bent into new angles, held tight, and then released. His pussy felt sore, and he knew it was the roughest sex he'd had in a long time despite not having an entirely clear memory of it.

There had been a dreamlike quality that Sam had surprisingly enjoyed despite not usually being comfortable with losing control like that. But it had been with Sebastian, and he knew that however vulnerable he was, Sebastian would never hurt or betray him. He was a good Dom. He was a good man.

Sam opened his eyes slowly, focusing on the man lying beside him in the bed.

He was just a man now, whereas the night before, he had been a god in the form of a swan. The evidence of that went beyond Sam's bruised body and to the end of the bed. There, long black gloves were draped, and on the dresser sitting on a velvet case, was an exquisite silver dildo shaped like a swan.

Sam couldn't help but huff a laugh and shake his head. Way too infatuated to pretend that Sebastian's level of eccentricity wasn't maddeningly appealing.

Sebastian started to stir, and Sam took his hand, smiling as he decided to continue the good king's fantasy. He pulled Sebastian's hand onto his lower belly, holding it there as he whispered, "Perhaps your seed has taken root, my king, but you should take me again, just in case it hasn't."

Sebastian woke with a groan as Sam grinned.

HeaLiNg TouCH

An accident on the ice reveals a secret.

Content Notes: Trans man/cis man.
Coming out, fear of rejection, injury, spell casting, monster, monster fucking, (magical) spit as lube, trans man topping cis man.
Anatomical References: Magical phalloplasty.

"The Third couple through this week and guaranteed a place on next week's Valentine's show is… John Jefferson and his skate partner Oliver Fontaine!"

The studio audience cheered and whooped, which made John grin. He wasn't entirely used to being popular or well-liked in real life, or more accurately – for being himself. But then, the audience – like his fans – only saw him on TV. This time it was as himself, not as a character. And perhaps the short interviews after performances and some of the training shoots presented him in a pleasant way. Not as the grumpy asshole he could often be, the one fans in the street had often labelled 'unapproachable'.

He glanced at Oliver, who had that barely-there smile that seemed controlled, curated. But he was smiling nonetheless; his chest puffed with modest pride.

John wondered if that was part of their appeal to the audience.

They were so mismatched in appearance and temperament that being one of the show's few same-sex couples to date was the least noteworthy thing about them. Oliver was on the shorter side, dark-skinned, stocky to the point of looking nothing like a professional figure skater's expected, delicate image. John was tall, athletic, and despite his dark hair, was so fair-skinned that any lighter he'd look ill. He looked more like a professional athlete than Oliver, with his chiselled jaw and masculine bearing, but equally looked like the daytime soap star he was.

Oliver was stoic but professional, no-nonsense but always pleasant. Whereas John had developed an easy-going persona for television, but in reality, he was guarded and aloof. He didn't know any other way to be, given his past.

Given what he'd had to do to get where he was, to be *who* he was.

And now they were going to be in the Valentine's Show. Incredible.

John's agent had been worried he was ageing out of the lead male roles and had deep concerns about upcoming contract negotiations for his continued appearance on *Days of Love*. But surely, making it this far and the spectacle of the Valentine Special would be enough to get him at least another year or two.

He *had* to. He simply didn't have anything else

in his life.

THree DayS Later

John looked at Oliver's arm and winced as they both made their way off the practice rink. The shoulder was dislocated; they were likely out of the competition even once the doctor treated it.

"I'm so sorry, Oliver," John said for the millionth time.

Oliver wouldn't have been overbalanced if he hadn't gotten his footing wrong as he moved into the lift. They wouldn't have landed on the hard ice so awkwardly, and Oliver wouldn't now be in pain whilst they made their way to the studio's infirmary.

This might be the end of it all.

From the moment they had met, John had enjoyed Oliver's company. It was refreshing to be around someone so down-to-earth and grounded. Someone who was natural around him and didn't treat him any differently for being a soap star. That wasn't something John had experienced much of for many years. People either loved him, or more accurately, his character, or disdained soap stars as not real actors.

John regretted that they didn't spend time with each other outside of the show and rehearsals. The times they were together were such a balm to John, such a break from the strange artificiality of his real life that he had come to treasure it. The last thing he wanted to do was cause Oliver any pain. And, selfishly, he didn't want to go out of the show early and never see Oliver again.

"Please, John. It's fine." Oliver gave him that reassuring smile that infuriated John –the one he used when John messed up a move. This had decreased over the weeks of the competition as John had improved, but this time it definitely wasn't fine.

This was a serious physical injury, and the way Oliver had said the words through gritted teeth made his pain clear. He winced as they sat down in the infirmary.

"Sorry," John repeated, placing a comforting hand on Oliver's thigh as the door opened and the doctor came in.

John had insisted on helping Oliver get home once the doctor had popped the dislocated shoulder back in and put his arm in a sling. He had to be off the ice for a few days and check in with the studio's physiotherapist. But it didn't look good. Technically a dislocated shoulder didn't have to knock him out of the show, but it was severe, and the final decision would be with the physio. They wouldn't want to risk long-term damage.

This might be the end of their time together.

Oliver lived in a modest city apartment, and whilst sparsely furnished, it was full of warm colours. The main focus of the lounge was a mahogany case filled with various trophies. And, notably, no signs of anyone else. No signs of a partner.

"You live alone?" John asked, followed immediately by, "I shouldn't leave you by yourself," without giving Oliver a chance to reply.

John chuckled nervously and stepped toward Oliver to help close the door behind them. Oliver thanked him despite wincing as they brushed against each other, though that same fond smile tweaked his lips.

"That was blunt," Oliver finally replied, amusement in his tone.

"Yeah, my foot likes to live in my mouth. I'm much better when they give me lines to say instead." John grimaced.

Oliver's smile was warm and comforting and instantly made John feel better.

Not for the first time, John realised.

In this more personal and comparatively intimate setting, he thought back on all their interactions so far and realised that perhaps they had become friends.

A thought that gave John his usual and instant reaction to people getting too close, he shuddered and stepped back. He knew no one would ever accept the real him and never wanted to put himself or others in the awkward situation of finding that out.

Oliver offered him a drink at the same time John said, "I should leave you to rest."

"No, please, you're more than welcome to stay. But... of course, if you must leave. If you have plans..."

John swallowed hard. He hadn't expected the disappointment in Oliver's tone or how he gazed at him, willing him to stay. Yes, perhaps they had become friends, but did Oliver want more?

"Oh, um, no. No plans. I just… you should rest." John tried to make excuses as he backed towards the apartment door as much as he wanted to stay.

They stood awkwardly for a moment with John's hand on the door handle before John needed to fill the silence and take his leave.

"I am sorry, Oliver. If I hadn't lost my footing…."

"John, please!" Oliver raised his voice, his expression instantly remorseful and, surprisingly, colour rose in his cheeks. "It was my fault."

John raised a brow in confusion. "How was it your fault? I tripped—"

"Yes, you did, but I could have… *should* have reacted in time to correct your fall and mine." Oliver sighed and then continued, mumbling, "I was distracted."

"By what?" John was still confused. It had just been them on the ice, no other distractions.

Oliver lowered his eyes, his cheeks so dark with a blush that John wondered if it was from the pain. He cleared his throat but continued to look at their feet.

"I have a confession," Oliver started, still not meeting John's eyes. "You see John… I have… been very fond of you – your character – since I happened upon *Days of Love*. In that first episode, when you saved the little girl from drowning in the lake… It's silly, I know. And I know that's not you; that's a character."

John couldn't help but nod despite Oliver not

looking up to see it.

"I had mixed feelings about being paired with you. I looked forward to getting to know you, but," Oliver finally met John's eyes, "I didn't know how to deal with my crush on you. I'm not usually one to fawn over celebrities."

Oliver chuckled again, but it was forced, self-conscious, and John shook his head.

"You've never fawned over me. I've always appreciated how down-to-earth you've been with me."

"I guess I'm a good actor too," Oliver rubbed the back of his neck awkwardly. "And I guess what I'm trying to admit is, uh," the following sentence came out in such a rush it was hard for John to take in, "for training, you were wearing a pair of sweats that bore a remarkable resemblance to a pair you wore in the episode *Love Loves Lovers*, and they were very flattering, then as now and I was… distracted. Momentarily."

As John digested the words, Oliver looked up, his expression hopeful.

"By my penis," John muttered, "distracted by my penis." He didn't realise he'd said it aloud until Oliver went wide-eyed, groaned, and nodded.

The irony.

"I shouldn't have said—" Oliver started, his blush even darker on his warm skin.

He looked beautiful.

"I can heal you," John blurted without thinking.

The sudden change in conversation threw Oliver as he now simply looked bewildered.

"I have a magical healing penis," John said

quickly, clapping his hand over his mouth for a moment before removing it to say, "I didn't mean to say that. I... I mean, I can help you. Get better. I can help heal you."

"With your penis?" Oliver's face was unreadable, stoic and cut off. After all the moments that, looking back, John could recognise as flirtation, this was the equivalent of shoving an unsolicited dick pic into the conversation.

"Um..." John mumbled, realising he'd probably overstayed his welcome.

Oliver's eyebrows slowly rose into his hairline as they both looked at each other in stunned silence.

John let out a heavy sigh, his shoulders dropping. He had never told anyone about this. It wasn't that it was prohibited, but he was stealth; he'd never wanted to disclose his trans status to anyone, much less everything else that came with it.

"John," Oliver's tone was as gentle as the hand he placed on John's arm, "I don't know what you're trying to—"

John stopped him with a shake of his head.

"I... have a condition." He started, unsure how to continue now that he had said it.

"A magical healing penis," Oliver replied, incredulous.

"Sort of," John winced, "I've never told anyone but... I owe you. If I hadn't distracted you."

"No, it's my fault," Oliver protested, but John continued undeterred, needing to say it aloud now that he had come this far.

"I wasn't born right. I didn't... have the right

parts," he looked at Oliver and then away, steeling himself to continue, "so I got them. I was poor then. Back when I was just a working-class kid from the middle of nowhere. I had no money for surgeries or hormones."

Oliver's eyes widened as John looked back up, clearly starting to understand.

"Believe it or not, I was a nerd. And I was into weird stuff; it was the early 2000s, and I was in probably half a dozen online covens. Some of them were more serious than others, techno-wicca. Anyway, someone gave me a spell or a conjuration. I didn't think it would work…."

Oliver blinked.

"You conjured a penis. That you could heal me with if you, I assume, fuck me."

Given the conversation, that shouldn't have irked John, but it did. Oliver wasn't dismissive, but it nonetheless played on John's insecurities. He had always planned to remain stealth, and this was a strange way to open up to someone. He wasn't sure he'd ever been this vulnerable before. But he was *definitely* sure it wasn't just because he felt guilty. He wanted Oliver to know.

He *wanted* Oliver.

And so his reaction, as simple as it was, stung.

John shrugged, "to put it crudely."

"Damn, sorry. I'm saying the wrong things," Oliver's hand on his arm rubbed up and down, a comforting gesture.

"I've never told anyone," John admitted.

He practically heard Oliver swallow before saying, "I'm honoured you decided to tell me."

There was a momentary silence between them until Oliver continued, "I like you, John. I think you know that. I think you can sense the compatibility between us. It's what allows us to skate together so well. I can't deny that I want you. But, I want you to want me. I don't want you to feel obligated—"

"Obligated!" John let out a bark of laughter.

"For injuring me. Or for being the distraction that caused me to injure myself," Oliver chuckled, tugging his arm and pulling John closer.

John's whole body trembled. Not just at the words but at the way Oliver gave him no room to consider being insecure about it, no room to run from him. All the same, it was unexpected when Oliver pressed him to the nearest wall and started grinding against him as they exchanged lustful gazes.

"Wait... wait..." John said, breathless as he pushed Oliver back. "I need to tell you... I mean, there's more. It's not just... my whole body changed. The spell wasn't just about having a magical penis. The magic is only present if I access the true form that the spell unleashed. This, what you see," John used his hands to indicate his body, the perfected form that had gotten him his career, "it's a facade. An illusion. I have to drop the illusion for the magic to work."

Oliver frowned, even as his hard cock remained pressed to John's hip.

"I'm not sure I understand," Oliver replied, and in that moment, John realised that perhaps Oliver didn't believe his farfetched and ridiculous tale. One so bizarre that it wouldn't even make it into the very worst episodes of *Days of Love*, of which there were already many.

There was only one course left; John would have to show him.

John let out a rumbling breath, unintentionally.

Before the spell, his voice had been high and feminine; after, in his human guise, it was deep and soft. In this form, it was almost beastly, and the last thing he wanted was to scare Oliver away.

"It's still me," John needlessly explained, as though Oliver hadn't just watched the illusion slip away and reveal his true form.

"You..." Oliver didn't seem scared; his voice had no tremble, and his eyes were wide with curiosity rather than fear. That much was clear from how his hand lingered in the air between them; he had started reaching out to touch and then stopped himself.

Likely because John was nearly naked now, only a loin cloth covered his impressive girth. Oliver's eyes roamed over him, taking in his duskier-than-usual skin tone, tinged with pink, especially the impressive horns that had sprouted from his forehead. His slight stubble was now a soft, shaggy beard; his eyes glowed red.

He remained still and let Oliver look his fill, unable to stop one of his long-furred ears from twitching, listening to every breath going in and out.

No, Oliver was definitely not afraid of him.

"So, you can heal me," Oliver said breathlessly.

"I can," John agreed, "with my penis."

"With your penis," Oliver repeated as he looked down at where John was starting to harden. "The penis you conjured…"

"It's part of me," John ran a large hand down his broad, muscled chest, resting just above his crotch, noting how Oliver tracked the movement. "I'm as male as you are. I always was on the inside, and now I am on the outside too."

Oliver nodded; it was difficult to disagree, "I'll say."

The words felt like an invitation: the words and the hungry look in Oliver's eyes.

"I'd have to penetrate you," John rumbled.

Oliver swallowed audibly. A loud gulp as he nodded and let his hand drift to John's chest.

"To heal me."

"Yes."

"I'd like that."

Minutes passed in a frenzy as their mouths met, and they pawed at each other. Oliver's clothes practically fell away under John's strong hands, and he had to remind himself to control his strength. He was meant to be healing Oliver, not roughing him up. As delightful as that might sound for another time.

Their urgent kisses broke so that Oliver could drag John to his bedroom; John's horns barely missed the door frame, which somehow made this whole thing so much more real. John hesitated next to the bed, drawing a concerned look from Oliver.

"John, I need you to know that were I not injured, were there not the possibility that this might keep us in the competition, I would still want you to fuck me right now."

John couldn't help the animalistic sound that escaped from his throat or the gathering of pre-come at the tip of his cock. If they both had the stamina for it, he'd want Oliver to fuck him too. He wanted everything. He wanted everything that Oliver would give him.

John swallowed, shaking as he processed Oliver's words and his own thoughts.

He never did this, had never *done* this. Not like this, not with the intent of healing someone. He'd only suspected it was possible when a masturbatory session had ended with a healed papercut. He probably should have read the small print on the spell before then, but he'd read it all now.

Not that the effects of his healing spunk were what stopped him from being intimate with people. It was much simpler than that. He had no desire to let anyone close, to reveal any of this about himself and his past. To out himself.

Not until Oliver. Not until today.

"Maybe once the competition is over," John trembled even as he panted the words, "we could see each other? A date... or not... um, friends at least, or..."

Oliver took the lead, pulling John to him as he had so many times whilst dancing on the ice. Though now he towered monstrously over him, Oliver didn't seem even slightly perturbed. "John, if I had my way, we'd have been dating for weeks."

John couldn't help the whimper or the tremble of his body as Oliver held him close. He could feel the weakness in Oliver's right arm even though he'd discarded the sling, and that brought him back to how this had all started.

"Maybe, I better make you well again first? Then we can see what happens." He managed to make the words somewhere between flirtatious and amused as he took hold of Oliver and gently laid him out on the bed, moving over him to take his mouth once more.

Ten minutes later, John had Oliver writhing beneath him as he opened him up with thick fingers, slicked from his own viscous and ample supply of saliva. Oliver laid back, John between his parted legs, his hips raised on a pillow, moaning with every touch.

"Is this okay?" John's voice rumbled low as he pressed kisses to Oliver's muscular, lightly furred thighs. Was this something Oliver had ever done before?

Bottoming generally, not specifically with a transgender, spell-made monster.

He didn't realise his hand had stilled until Oliver pushed back against him to take his fingers deep. Maybe he had done this before?

"Is this good, Oliver? Does it feel good?" John asked, a balance of nerves and arousal as he controlled himself enough not to be rough.

Oliver moaned his affirmative answer.

"You like to be fucked?" John encouraged. "You've done this before..." It wasn't a question as he began moving his fingers again, feeling Oliver relax into the motion.

"I have. Never with... someone like you." Oliver

admitted before his words became a moan. John was more than happy to know Oliver was aroused by his form, but he still felt a hollowness that he hadn't expected.

Oliver's cock was twitching as John pumped his fingers harder and deeper.

"I want you to take me, John." Oliver groaned and pushed down on John's fingers again. "I want to feel what it's like to be fucked by you. By a beautiful self-made man."

John stilled, desire and warmth blossoming in his chest. That was what he needed, he realised. Acceptance of who he was as a trans man, not just his true form. He loved his body and himself and would cast that spell again if he had to. But there was something so deeply satisfying that Oliver saw past the surface and wanted him for who he truly was.

John scooched forward, taking his fingers from Oliver as he did so and clutching for balance on the skater's thick thighs. All hesitation gone, John's hard, girthy cock pressed against Oliver's ass, and they both sighed with relief as he breached.

Oliver groaned as John slowly inched inside, pulling back out to spit down onto his cock, spreading it with his hand before pushing back inside as Oliver arched beneath him.

"Yes," he hissed breathlessly, "fuck me, John."

Those words made John growl, but instead of giving in to the roughness, he pulled back slowly before pushing back in with equal patience. He moved like that a few more times before leaning over Oliver, mindful not to put any pressure on his injured arm. John held himself just above Oliver, his hips working at an ever-increasing pace as he leaned in for a kiss. It was messy and wet as neither of them could give their mouths focus, their minds and bodies too absorbed elsewhere.

They groaned against each other's lips when Oliver wrapped his legs around John, his heels urging him deeper. John's groans turned to grunts, and Oliver huffed a little noise of pleasure on each thrust, building to a crescendo as John went quicker and deeper.

Then Oliver groaned long and low and went pliant beneath him.

"There… there, John…" Oliver whimpered as John railed his prostate. Oliver went slack, but for his legs which gripped firmly to John's waist, allowing John to pound into him with abandon.

"I'm gonna…." John cried out as he came inside Oliver, no longer caring if his sperm fixed the skater's injury, only caring about their release.

John straightened up a little, pulling away from Oliver enough to see that the man had streaked his belly and chest with come. They studied each other for a long moment before John pulled back, slowly withdrawing from Oliver as they groaned at the sensation before he flopped down on the bed beside him.

Oliver rolled to face him, instantly cupping a hand to John's beastly face and pulling him in for a kiss. They kissed until they couldn't breathe any more, breaking apart and panting hot against each other's skin.

"Thank you, John," Oliver managed, breathless,

"I feel much better already."

John wasn't sure what time they had fallen asleep in the end; he only knew that it was after they had fucked a few more times, just to be sure.

Within a few hours, Oliver's arm was completely pain-free and recovered, so much so that he could hold John's weight as he pinned him against the kitchen wall and fucked him hard in return. Then there had been some rather enjoyable blowjobs at the dining table, followed by a return to the bedroom and Oliver begging John to fuck his ass again. Again, just to be sure that the injury really had healed.

They fell asleep fresh from a shared bath, cradled together in tangled bed sheets, wrapped in each other's soapy scent. Oliver's head pillowed against John's expansive, soft chest.

It was the phone that woke them.

Oliver reached over and picked it up, spooning against John. John sighed his contentment and snuggled back.

"Hello?" Oliver's voice was thick with sleep. John could hear a muttering on the other end of the line but not the actual words. "I see. Thanks," were the only words uttered before Oliver hung up the phone.

Silence hung between them, and John's concern only dissipated when Oliver began to stroke one of his long, furry ears absentmindedly.

"That was the physio," Oliver started; John

repositioned to look at him as he continued, "She, uh, said I should be fine to continue. She was happy with the doctor's report and thinks I should be right as rain. Though she suggested you do any lifts for the next couple of weeks."

Silence fell again as Oliver rolled back, and they lay side by side, looking up at the ceiling.

"So, there was no need for us to…" John trailed off and swallowed.

"No. No, I guess not." Oliver agreed. After a beat, he rolled his shoulder and stretched his arm, wincing audibly. "That said, it couldn't hurt to go back out there in peak condition. And my arm still feels a bit stiff."

John sucked in a breath, unable to regret or even be sorry about what happened, considering what it had led to. Oliver cocked a brow at him and grinned as John surged up and pushed him back on the bed, caging him there.

"Stiff arm, huh?" John growled, grinding their hard shafts together, "That isn't the only thing that's stiff."

POWErFUL Dangerous

T4T is pretty magical. And potentially dangerous.

Content Notes: Trans man/trans woman.
Magic, references to past parent death, dark sense of humour, joking about death, references to misuse of power.
Anatomical References: PIV penetration. Cock used for trans female genitalia. Cock, hole, pussy, t-cock, and dick used for trans male genitalia.

Freya Woodsmoke sipped at her wine, wishing it was whiskey. But if trying to pick up in taverns had taught her anything, people expected women to be ladylike, which meant wine, for some damned reason.

It really was awful and lacked the comforting burn of whiskey, but that could wait until she was home. Unless she got lucky.

The idea seemed laughable, given that it happened so rarely. In the two years since she'd started her coven training at the Blackthorn Academy, she could count on one hand the number of times she'd picked up in a tavern. In truth, sex wasn't high on her priorities, but sometimes she just had an itch that needed scratching, and so she came to what, she was pretty sure, was the only queer tavern in the whole area. And most of the time, she struck out.

Maybe she was just too picky? Or probably just too wary. It was most likely because she always came across as awkward and standoffish.

It didn't help that she wasn't always in the mood to go home with a woman, and trying to find a guy into women at a gay bar when – even if they were bi – they were likely there for dick, too, was difficult. The existence of binaries was irksome, as all spellcasters knew. After all, good and evil as a binary concept was older than any of the covens, and the common humans clung to it.

Freya slugged back the wine, forgetting for a moment that it wasn't whiskey and almost retched. She took a moment to compose herself and willed her face not to turn inside out, thanks to the sourness that followed. And then she pushed her glass away and decided it was time to call it a night.

When she turned on her barstool to get up, the next stool along from her was now occupied by another lone drinker. She stopped and studied him.

He seemed tall, though it was hard to tell with them both seated. His features were angular, and his lips full. He was very nice to look at, to say the least.

"Can I help you?" He turned to her and asked with a smirk.

She blushed and held her hand over her eyes at being caught out, feeling the heat creep up her neck.

"Shit, sorry. I've had a glass of wine, and... you're kinda distracting." Freya was caught in her usual social ineptitude of somewhere between rude and flirtatious – usually dependent on how the other person reacted.

"Thanks, I think." Like silk, the man's words were smooth in a heavily accented rumble that made Freya quiver. "Can I buy you another glass of wine?"

"Um… sure," Freya replied. "Actually, no. I mean, the wine is terrible. Wait, a whiskey."

The man's smile grew, and she realised he was finding her charming, which was fantastic news! Now, as long as he wasn't exclusively into men, she might be in with a chance.

He flagged down the bartender and ordered a whiskey for Freya and a wine for himself before turning back to her.

"Wine is often an acquired taste."

"Pfft," Freya replied to the frankly somewhat patronising words. "On your head be it then. Hope you got something better than the house white because that stuff is awful."

The smiling didn't falter, and he offered his hand to shake, "Theo Linseed."

An interesting name, she noted. Linseed wasn't a common surname in these parts, though his accent already marked him as foreign.

"Freya Woodsmoke, Freya." Freya offered, taking Theo's hand and enjoying the feel of skin against skin more than she possibly should. "Are, uh… Are you at the Academy too?"

"No, I'm on a different track. I'm studying scientific medicine at the human university." There were no human universities for at least two cities, so it made more sense when Theo continued, "I'm just here visiting a friend." He nodded towards the dancefloor, where Freya saw a fellow Blackthorn student engrossed with the beautiful redhead she was swaying with. "But she seems to have found better company."

"Ah," Freya replied. "Well, I can keep you company." She attempted to be flirty, hoping it didn't stray too far into creepy.

"I'd like that," Theo replied.

There was a moment of silence as they regarded each other, and Freya felt the blush on her cheeks under his unwavering gaze. He really was ridiculously attractive.

"So," she cleared her throat and nodded towards the fellow Blackthorn, "how do you two know each other?"

From his accent, he was from across the Green Sea, but she was sure no one in her coven was. Freya's investigative mind was immediately curious about how they would have met and whether there was any history there. She ignored the slight bite of jealousy in her gut. It was a ridiculous response given they had just met, and this might go nowhere.

"We briefly attended the same girl's academy when I first came across the Green Sea and became fast friends. We have remained so over the years."

Freya frowned, sure she hadn't misheard but queried nonetheless, "Girl's school?"

Theo's smile was soft and open, "yes, is that a problem?"

Freya felt her blush back again, her cheeks felt hot as it clicked, and she stammered, "No, no, not at all. No…"

"Good," Theo replied with a low rumble as he picked up his glass and watched her over the rim of it as he drank.

Damn, Freya was starting to get hard. This guy was absolutely magnetic, charming and—

"And you're here alone?" Theo asked, his tone innocent but his eyes burning into hers.

She swallowed and nodded, "Yeah, just came to unwind after a long day."

He smirked at her, and a raised brow told her he knew she was fibbing.

"And maybe try to get laid," she admitted and chuckled. There was something strangely enjoyable about how he seemed to see right through her.

Maybe it was the horrible wine and the excellent whiskey, but Freya found it hard to deny the connection she was feeling.

"Ah," Theo acknowledged with a grin, "any good prospects?"

This was where she could cheesily say, not until you walked in, or something equally awful. But instead, she said, "That depends."

Theo shuffled on his stool, moving a little closer to her, their knees brushing as he leaned in and asked softly, "Depends on what?"

"How you feel about this," she said as she took one of his hands and placed it flat on her knee before running it up over her skirt to her crotch. She never tucked when she came to this place, but she wore somewhat restrictive panties. All the same, her half-hard cock was impossible not to pass as anything else with a hand directly upon it.

"I feel just fine about it," Theo's reply was breathless and muttered almost against her lips. They both leaned in just a little, enough for their mouths to meet in a gentle but open kiss. Freya moaned as Theo's tongue slipped inside her mouth, and his hand gently massaged her growing bulge.

When they broke apart, Freya was panting as she said, "I live within walking distance, and my covenmates are out."

Theo smirked and rose from his stool.

The lodging had two bedrooms; Freya's housemates Clara and Atlantia shared one room, having been a couple since before they came to the Academy.

Therefore, Freya's room was smaller but more than adequate, with a double bed and dimly lit by several well-placed jars of lightning bugs. Atlantia teased her about how perfect it could be as a hook-up pad; she just wished she got to use it as such more often.

Not a regret she was having this evening as Theo walked her backwards towards her bed.

A gracious host, she had offered him a drink as soon as they'd arrived, but he had declined and instead asked to use the bathroom. Whilst he was freshening up, Freya went to her room and took off her shirt, leaving just the satin camisole beneath. When he'd come looking for her, she hadn't objected to him coming into her room. It was, after all, why they were there.

And now she found the back of her legs hitting

the bed as Theo's arms went around her waist to stop her from falling.

"You're beautiful," Theo breathed the words just above her mouth before capturing her lips in a soft, exploratory kiss.

When they drew back from each other, Freya shook her head, "I probably taste like bad wine."

"You taste perfect, and the wine wasn't so terrible," Theo murmured, pressing his nose against her and stealing little pecks as he lowered them both to the bed.

"It's ridiculous. I hate wine. I only drink it because that's what women drink."

Theo pulled back and looked at her then, his gaze full of affection and understanding, it was overwhelming, but she couldn't break the intense eye contact.

"Wine is an acquired taste," he told her softly, "bad wine can put you off forever. I don't believe that your genitals come into it."

That made Freya laugh and shake her head, finally breaking the intense moment.

"I suppose not. But you know what I mean."

"Yes, I do." Theo agreed.

Freya pulled him down into a hungry kiss; their bodies pressed together.

Theo broke away as he slid his hand down to Freya's hard cock.

"What should I call this?" Theo murmured the words over her mouth.

"Cock is fine," she replied, breathless as he squeezed her gently.

"Same for me," he told her.

"Do you want—"

"What do you like to—"

They started simultaneously and then subsided into another chuckle and more hungry kisses.

Freya shuddered as Theo kissed down her neck and to her chest, nosing at a nipple through her camisole.

"Is this okay?" He asked, to which she enthusiastically nodded and groaned as he sucked the nipple into his mouth through the thin material. No one had ever read her body so well before.

"Do you like to use your cock?" Theo asked as he continued to massage it and lick at her nipple.

"Yeah…" Freya panted. "Do you like to, um…."

"Yes," Theo replied, making his point by grinding his crotch on her thigh. "Sheaths?"

"Y-yeah…" Freya felt a shiver over her skin as she shuffled slightly, moving across the bed to reach for the bedside drawer. Theo moved with her and leaned over to reach in when she opened the drawer, pulling out what they needed.

They kissed again, pecks and deep kisses interspersed before finally finding the strength to pull away from each other completely.

Theo stepped off the bed and began removing his clothes, his eyes not leaving her body as she did the same. The way he watched her made her all the harder, his eyes roaming over every inch of revealed flesh.

First, she removed her camisole and then pushed down her skirt, pulling off her socks and shoes and finally lying back in just her panties. Her cock strained against the binding underwear, ever more so as she, in turn, watched Theo.

He undid his shirt slowly and let it fall to the floor, revealing an athletic build and wonderfully furred chest. His pants and underwear quickly followed until he stood entirely naked, his small cock peeking between his equally furred crotch and thighs.

"Fuck," Freya gasped the word as she drank him in.

That earned her a smirk as he began to advance on her. The closer he drew, the further she spread her legs until he was between them, his hand rubbing gently against her panties.

"Can I take these off?" He asked softly.

Freya nodded with enthusiasm as her cheeks heated.

Theo smiled as he spread his hands across her hips and hooked his fingers into her panties, pulling them smoothly down until her cock sprang free.

"Fuck," Freya muttered again, more turned on than she was sure she ever had been before.

She'd expected a quick fumble and fuck, but this was sensual and intimate.

"Will you let me be on top?" Theo asked her, his voice a low husk that made her shiver and nod.

"Tell me if you want to stop, if I do anything you don't like," Theo said as he pushed her legs back gently, leaving her cock free and erect.

She took hold of her legs and held them as Theo released them and instead took her cock in hand. He stroked it a few times, his touches a caress as he rolled the sheath down her shaft and then reached over for the oil. He squeezed some onto her before stroking his hand up and down, coating her thoroughly from root to tip.

The sensation had Freya curling her toes. His hand felt so good on her, like he'd read a manual specifically on the best way to get her off. She wasn't even sure she needed more than this; a hand job sounded pretty fantastic in itself.

But then Theo's hand was gone, and he moved up until he was over her, practically straddling her.

Freya blinked, confused and unsure what Theo was trying to do until he lowered himself.

They both moaned as Freya slipped inside Theo's slick hole. It was a slow motion, but even so, within moments, Theo had taken all of her and closed his eyes in bliss.

Freya closed her eyes then, too, scrunching them together and trying not to come.

The feeling was intense, and seeing how much Theo also enjoyed it was almost too much.

Theo settled for a moment, and Freya wondered if he was having the same problem as she was. If he was crazy close to coming too. When he finally moved, he repositioned ever so slightly, and Freya winced. Theo was now sat in such a way that Freya's cock was pointing downwards more than was usual. It didn't hurt, and the slight discomfort passed quickly, but it was strange. A completely different sensation than she was used to.

This whole evening seemed to be full of discoveries.

And then Theo began to move.

"Oh fuck!" Freya tensed momentarily, her abs pulling taut until she grew used to the movements, to Theo fucking her.

Because that's what it felt like.

She'd had people ride her dick before, and this wasn't that. This felt like their positions were flipped and roles reversed – as though Theo had the cock and he was fucking into her pussy.

"Is this okay?" Theo asked without slowing down or stopping. He continued to pump his hips. Between Theo's wetness and the lube, Freya could feel the slick slide of their bodies and words were gone, only leaving her with the ability to nod.

Panting, Theo repositioned slightly again; he was kneeling behind her now, the front of his thighs pressed against the back of hers as his hands went down to her inner thighs to hold her legs up and open.

"Oh god, Theo!"

He moved.

He really was fucking her now. Thrusting himself hard and fast on her cock, pounding her into the mattress.

Freya was already so close, so turned on, that the sight of him was almost enough to push her over the edge. His gaze was hungry but tender as he fucked her, his fingers stroking her inner thighs gently even as he pressed them down with unquestionable strength.

Freya wanted this again and again.

She wanted Theo again and again.

"You feel so good," Theo growled, making Freya's cock throb all the more.

Something Theo must have felt because he moaned and clenched around her.

"So do you," Freya gasped, unable to stop herself from reaching down and pressing her fingers against his t-cock.

She just had to feel him; needed to be grounded by it.

Her fingers were instantly wet with the mixture of lube and both their juices as she slid her fingers on either side of his cock and began to rub, jerking him off in time with his thrusts.

"Yesss," Theo hissed.

And that was when she saw him crack.

All this evening, when they were flirting, when they were kissing, even when they were fucking, he retained some level of calm stoicism. His enjoyment was obvious, and there was no doubt about that. He wasn't holding back. But it suddenly felt like there was a crack in his armour, and magic was threatening to break through.

"I'm going to—" he started, but the words ended in a grunt as she felt him throb between her fingers.

Freya's eyes rolled with pleasure as the throbbing was mirrored by the clenching of his inner muscles, working her cock until she came with a groan.

It was sudden, like a shot of electricity through her, while having been worked up to feverishly. It left her whole body feeling raw and oversensitive as she emptied herself inside him. Her control almost breaking.

Both of them were shaking, sweating and panting when they stopped coming.

Freya was in a daze as Theo let her legs go and then moved up her, kissing her softly as he finally let her slide from him, sheath and all.

Freya vaguely sensed it being removed, and then Theo pulled her into his arms and their bodies entwined around each other in the most intense post-coital bliss Freya had ever felt.

Freya woke when her alarm went off, immediately setting it to snooze before rolling over to get another twenty minutes.

Rolling over was more difficult than expected when she realised her evening's conquest was still there. And what's more, she didn't mind one bit.

Usually, hook-ups – when they did happen – were just that, one-night stands. To scratch that itch, nothing more. They usually parted ways once the sex was over.

But last night?

Freya had never been this close to losing control before. It was the first thing everyone learned, walk, talk, control. At times in her life, she'd been angry, upset or even euphoric and never lost control. Never even came close or believed it could be of any concern. And last night she nearly had, and she knew Theo had been close too.

She watched him sleep, drinking in every inch of his beauty and wishing they could do this again and again.

It was a terrible idea.

Being so compatible as to shake each other's control was dangerous. There was no telling what might happen if one or both lost control of their magic, even for moments.

It really was a terrible idea. It was irresponsible but… so hard to resist.

She shifted in the bed, and when Theo didn't stir, Freya took the opportunity to slot herself against him, resting her head on his furred chest and pressing her stiffening morning wood against his thigh.

In a seemingly automatic gesture, his arm came up around her and held her close, but she realised he had started to stir when his breathing changed, and he rested his chin in her hair. Then he nuzzled into it and took a deep breath.

"I probably stink!" Freya protested with a chuckle, normalcy returning in the most oppressive way.

Theo murmured, his voice thick with sleep, "I can smell the dry ice from the bar, your natural scent of sweat and sex, and beneath it, the delicate peach blossom of your shampoo."

"Sounds gross," Freya dismissed, chuckling again at this absolutely delightful weirdo she'd brought home.

"On the contrary, you smell as you are – beautiful."

Even as her chest warmed, Freya scoffed, an automatic reaction, "Are you always this sappy?"

"Only when appropriate. If you'd rather I say no more or, indeed, leave, I will do so."

"No," Freya protested quicker than she'd meant to, knowing she shouldn't. She should let him go, and he surely knew that too. *We should talk about this*, she thought, though the words were harder to come by.

"Hmm," Theo looked down at her and hooked a finger under her chin, "we needn't speak at all for now."

Freya's breath hitched; she'd never had her thoughts read before. They really could be something truly remarkable together.

They leaned together, and their lips met in a gentle press that made Freya tingle all over, the magic between them a static buzz. There was a slow, desperate consumption to the kiss like they would eat each other or crawl inside one another if they possibly could.

Instead, they settled for moving their bodies together, Theo rocking against her so their dicks frot together to create an exquisite friction. A wonderful slide as both grew wetter until another climax gripped them. Less powerful this time but still the same potential for control to slip. She knew it shouldn't, but it sent a thrill through Freya.

They breathed together for a few moments before Theo rolled off of her, and they lay side by side on the bed, both trying to catch their breath. A comfortable silence that seemed to envelop Freya in warmth surrounded them. They lay like that for a long time.

The air between them crackled. Electricity sparked along their goosepimpled flesh, where parts of them almost touched.

Finally, Freya cleared her throat, "we shouldn't do this."

"I know," Theo replied, his voice deep and laced with concern. "But I don't know that I care." He rolled onto his side to face her. "Maybe our meeting was fate. This connection, I know you can feel it. The right thing, the sensible thing, would be to step away. But selfishly, I don't think I want to. I have had too much taken from me to give up things I want."

Freya trembled at the strength of his words and the power behind his declaration. Whatever might come of this thing between them, he had deemed it something he needed to explore to the nth. It was already eating at her fast-diminishing resolve.

"Theo was my father's name, a family name," he muttered quietly as his fingers moved to Freya's lithe belly, running over her flesh until sparks crackled at the contact. "It would have been my name if I had been acknowledged as male at birth. It felt like something that should be mine, especially after my parents passed."

"I'm sorry," Freya placed her hand gently over his. This was dangerous, she kept repeating in her mind, but could she be something else he lost? Did she want to be?

"Don't be sorry. You didn't kill them." She could hear the smile in his voice.

"Shit, you're dark," Freya was shocked and amused as she pulled back to look at him. "I kinda like it."

"I too, am an acquired taste." Theo smiled at her, breaking the tension.

"I think I like you a lot more than I like bad wine," Freya laughed, feeling her cheeks heat under his smiling gaze.

He pushed a lock of hair behind her ear and

nuzzled into her neck, making her shudder again when he told her, "I think I like you a lot more than many, many things."

Freya tried to hesitate, tried to resist him, one last attempt at it. Her mind reeled with examples of past folk who had been unable to control their magic: the death and destruction, the power and potential to give in to desires. Taking anything and everything you wanted was too easy if no one could stop you. And yet, even as she hesitated, a thrill ran through her at the thought. What could they become together? What powerful creatures might they transform into?

"We shouldn't. It's dangerous," even to her own ears, the words didn't sound sincere. "This connection... we could—"

"We could become the most powerful people in the world."

"The most dangerous," Freya added, though any lingering concern floated from her like ash rising from a raging fire. Behind Theo's eyes, that same fire blazed.

ALIENS

&

ANdroids

Inappropriate Thoughts

Tom can't stop dreaming about his oversized boyfriend.

Content Notes: Human trans man/alien cis male. Alien sex, size difference, huge alien penis, just the tip.
Anatomical References: PIV penetration. Vagina, pussy, erection, and cock used for trans male genitalia.

Tom woke with a strange metallic taste in his mouth and a painfully hard erection.

A clear indication that he'd had another dream about his boyfriend, the ship's gilesean medical officer. He turned his head and groaned into the pillow, practically assaulted by the flood of images of everything he'd ever wanted Rigal to do to him. The fantasy of being fucked over his workstation in engineering was a titillating sort of obscene that was doing nothing to quell his arousal.

It had been almost exactly six months since their relationship had become intimate.

Sexual.

As difficult as that could be between a human and a gilesean.

Some encounters were much easier than others.

Tom enjoyed the casual intimacy they had acquired. He liked feeling wanted, loved. He liked the mornings when they woke in each other's arms and the nights when Rigal curled his massive body around him. Most of the time, he'd say he liked that more than the sex. Sex he could live without, but the comfort of someone being there for him in the cold of space was something he needed.

But sometimes, Tom was desperate for Rigal's touch. Including the sort that they didn't dare even attempt. It left him horny and frustrated and resulted in painfully hard morning erections and an unfathomably wet pussy.

Tom knew when this had all first started that penetrative sex wasn't going to happen, as much as he sometimes thought he might be willing to die trying.

Death being the most likely outcome should they attempt it.

There was simply no way a gilesean penis would fit inside a human vagina without some horrific damage. Not that it stopped Tom from craving it.

Possessing just under double the average mass of humans, gileseans could only be described as robust. Thick. All over.

Tom was a large bear of a guy, and Rigal dwarfed him in a way that only deepened his arousal.

It was some compensation that Rigal gave the best blowjobs Tom had ever experienced. Feeling the sharp gilesean teeth graze over his small shaft, that threat of something a little dangerous was an undeniable turn-on.

And from Rigal's reactions, Tom was sure he wasn't too bad at reciprocating either, though it wasn't so much deep-throating as sucking on the tip like a lollipop whilst he stroked the rest with two firm hands.

Sometimes they would rut together, their incredibly different cocks rubbing together until they were slick with each other's emissions. Lips locked in a deep kiss as they grunted and humped and came copiously between their tightly pressed bodies.

So, it was primarily blowjobs and hand jobs, both of which, with varying levels of intimacy depending on the situation, was more than adequate for Tom.

Usually.

With a sigh, Tom slid a hand into his underwear and pressed his fingers on either side of his cock, stroking as he let the dream flood back to him as he imagined Rigal fucking into him as he bent over his workstation.

Tom sat beside Rigal in a quiet corner of the mess hall, Rigal's massive hand resting lightly on Tom's thigh as they sipped coffee on their mid-morning break. This was what Tom needed, what he liked. He didn't *need* sex, not even when the sudden and unbidden thoughts of last night's dream flashed into his mind and had his cock filling.

"Do you ever... um... No, never mind." The words had fallen out before Tom had even fully formed them. He stopped and cursed his dreams.

"Tom?" Rigal frowned down at him.

Tom sucked in a breath.

"In the spirit of honesty," Tom started. How many times had they used that phrase in the last six months? In the spirit of honesty, Rigal, I wouldn't say I like your attempts at cooking earth food. In the spirit of honesty, Rigal, I prefer fewer teeth on my nipples.

"In the spirit of honesty, do you ever think about, um, fucking me? I've been thinking about it, dreaming about it."

Rigal's eyebrows shot up so fast that Tom was amazed he didn't fall off his chair with the momentum. If Rigal were a cartoon, they would have left his face entirely whilst he made an audible gulp. Instead, Rigal lowered his eyebrows back into place, righted his expression and cleared his throat.

"It's not a possibility," Rigal replied and sipped at his coffee, looking away as though to end the conversation.

"That's not what I asked," Tom replied with a huff, but Rigal didn't respond, staying silent until the whistle sounded for the miners to get back to the refinery decks.

After their coffee together, and specifically the conversation they hadn't really had, Tom didn't expect to see Rigal after work that night.

He clocked off his shift and returned to his quarters, anticipating that they might ignore each other for a few days and then return to normal, as when they'd had slight disagreements previously. Perhaps not the healthiest way to do things, but there were only so many ways to function in relationships when stuck on a mining ship, three solar systems from home.

Tom thought the time alone would allow him to clear his head of the dream haunting him all day. But instead, it had just given him time and space to think – to imagine. The images in the dream were burned into his mind, so it was all too easy to imagine Rigal pushing him up against the wall or pinning him down on the bed. All too *damn* easy to imagine being fucked over the small personal workstation in his quarters.

It wasn't long before Tom was so on edge and needing release that he considered going to Rigal anyway. He could apologise, and they could have a make-up sixty-nine.

"Tom?" Rigal's voice sounded through the comms box at Tom's door, and it was almost enough to make him come in his jumpsuit.

Knowing there was no point in trying to compose himself, Tom pressed for the door to open, and Rigal quickly stepped inside, rubbing a hand over the back of his neck and looking sheepish.

"I think this is my fault," Rigal winced as he spoke.

"What is?" Tom frowned, caught off guard and a little confused.

"I have been thinking about what it would be like to penetrate you, and I believe those thoughts may have, um, infiltrated yours."

"You've implanted thoughts? In my head?" Tom was flummoxed.

"No, no. It's more like osmosis. But not between plants. Between lovers. It's common on Gilese. Where there is intimacy, this can happen. Often accompanied by a metallic taste in the mouth."

"Not all of us are medical officers, Doctor!" Tom challenged, bewildered by the turn of events, "It might have been nice to know about these sorts of things when we first started dating."

Rigal winced again and offered an apologetic glance, "I had no idea it would happen with a human."

"So… my inappropriate thoughts are actually *your* inappropriate thoughts." Tom huffed, folding his arms across his broad chest.

"I suppose it depends on how you feel about them," Rigal said, trying to sidestep responsibility for Tom's horniness.

"I feel like I want you to fuck me! How do you feel about them?" Tom challenged in a gruff tone, the tension between them.

Rigal let out a soft sigh, appearing totally composed.

Contrarily, Tom's mouth was dry, and his throat ached as his cock pressed hard against the confines of his tight pants.

"Rigal," Tom breathed out his lover's name and closed the space between them, gently sliding his hand over Rigal's hip.

Rigal cleared his throat, a betrayal from beneath his calm demeanour, they both knew. Tom was tempted to look down and see whether Rigal's jumpsuit now had a tent that mirrored his much smaller bulge, but he knew he didn't have to.

"Tom—" Rigal breathed out his name and raised a hand to his face. Tom leaned into it. Rigal's hand slipped from his cheek and around his neck, jerking him sharply into a hungry kiss. And then Rigal moved him to his workstation, positioning him so that Tom almost sat on it. Tom returned the kiss, teeth and tongue fighting with passion as his hands went to Rigal's jumpsuit and began undoing the belt. Rigal mirrored the action moments later, pulling Tom forward again by his belt, his large hands fumbling.

Even so, Tom's jumpsuit was stripped off his shoulders and pushed down along with his underwear. Rigal's own were pulled to his thighs when he grabbed Tom roughly and turned him, forcing him to the desk.

Tom went with a gasp but didn't resist. He moaned as he was pushed down. "Yes, Rigal… please fuck me…"

That seemed to bring Rigal back to his senses, and he stopped suddenly. His large, firm hand on Tom's back, holding him down, eased off and began caressing gently.

"I'll not injure you."

"I… I just…" Tom felt desperate. He wanted something, needed it. He wanted Rigal, but he knew that it really was impossible.

A moment passed, both panting but otherwise quiet; Tom still bent to the workstation with everything exposed.

And then Rigal's hands grabbed his hips

roughly, and Tom released a gasp, more of anticipation than of shock. He went pliant, allowing Rigal to push him to the workstation again.

"Open your legs wider." The tone was soft but thick with lust.

Tom felt a tremble through him and a pull of anticipation and anxiety in his gut. Were they going to do this?

"What…" the word was moaned out at the sensation of Rigal pressing against him and then sliding his huge cock between Tom's thighs.

"Close your legs, Tom…."

Tom could feel Rigal's cock press right up against him; just shy of pushing into him, he slid through, pressing firmly against Tom's cock. It took him a moment to get his thoughts together, and then he did as he was told and clenched his thighs as tight together as he could around the massive member, causing a gasp from Rigal.

And then Rigal moved.

"Oh fuck!" The words escaped from Tom's mouth, and his body went limp across the workstation, moving with Rigal's body as he fucked between his thighs.

It wasn't penetration, but it was… it was something, and it didn't feel like a compromise. Tom couldn't describe the satisfaction he felt; nothing could come close to the act of having another person's hard cock sliding between your thighs – causing friction against your slick cock and pussy.

Rigal was pressed tight to him, their skin flush against each other.

Tom was letting out gasps and moans, feeling close to the edge and overwhelmed by the new and unexpected stimulation as the underside of his cock was dragged against Rigal's with every movement.

He cried out in surprise when Rigal reached a hand around and slid his large fingers against Tom's slick cock. The slide of Rigal's cock pressing against him with each thrust was in time with the rhythm Rigal set with his hand. He felt surrounded by the man in a way he only ever had with others when there was penetration.

The sensation was overwhelming, and Tom felt his legs go weak as though they might give way. To counter this, he squeezed his thighs as tight as possible, drawing a guttural noise from Rigal.

"Tom…" The gilesean moaned his name as he thrust harder, over and over. Each thrust pressed insistently against Tom's pussy until finally, with a deep groan that shook them both, Rigal squeezed barely the very tip of his cock into Tom as he came.

Tom cried out at the sensation, the stretch and feeling of being filled as Rigal's come pumped into him so copiously that it began to leak back out. It was enough to send him over the edge until he was coming too, squeezing around the Rigal's tip.

With a grunt, Tom collapsed onto the workstation, Rigal covering him completely and pinning him there even as he tried to hold his full weight off the smaller man.

Tom's undershirt was uncomfortably rumpled and partially covered in his come. He needed to move but wasn't sure his legs would work. He felt wrecked in the very best way.

"That was…" Tom panted out.

"Intercrural." Rigal supplied.

"I was going to say amazing." Tom chuckled lightly. "I've never… I didn't even…" He was unsure how to voice the feeling of discovery. As though they two were the first ever to experience this act.

Tom chuckled again and considered how messy and uncomfortable it would be for them to go, jumpsuits around ankles from the workstation to his bathroom.

His thoughts were broken when he realised Rigal was hardening again, as his kind could frustratingly do.

"Rigal…?" Tom started, only to find his mind flooded with images, an instant replay of everything they had just done and an unmistakable sense of Rigal's desire to do it again immediately.

He could taste the thoughts like a metallic tang at the back of his tongue.

He found he liked it.

Kyanite

Chase might be falling for his best customer.

Content Notes: Human trans man/alien cis male.
Camboy, sex work, sex toys, live sex stream,
hemipenes, double penetration, double penetration
in two holes, front hole penetration, masturbation,
anal sex.
Anatomical References: PIV penetration. Front
hole, cock, t-cock used for trans male genitalia.

This wasn't how Chase had intended to put himself
through medical school, but as high-paying jobs
went, this was a pretty enjoyable option. It might
have been different if his parents hadn't decided to
become mining prospectors and moved them all to
an outer planet. When the bubble burst, and the
chances of returning to a core planet evaporated,
Chase knew he'd never get a job with the wages
he'd need for tuition. He was just lucky that he
wasn't on a planet even further out that he wouldn't
even be able to access the immersive study
programme. He was lucky he got to pursue his
dream of medicine at all.

Even so, when it came to live-streaming sexual
content every night for credits, he found a strange
pleasure in it. There was something gratifying about

people paying such ridiculously high credits for something so simple as a wank.

When he fucked himself on a toy? As credits dropped into his account, the sound of pings was almost deafening.

Chase had initially felt weird at the thought of being fetishised by those who might watch him specifically because he was trans. Those who tuned in just because one day he might be wanking off his prosthetic cock, and another he might be riding considerable dildos in one or both holes. But the credits swayed him. If that was how people got their rocks off, the least he could do was exploit them and their credit accounts for the troubles.

Chase stretched out on his bed, feline-like, in front of the recording screen. The now wet and sticky dildo he'd just pulled out of his well-used front hole lay discarded on the bed next to him. He continued to make a show of his recovery from absolute debauchery until the dings of the credits started to slow, and his audience dissipated.

After another long stretch, Chase sat up and typed into the tablet linked to the screen.

:: Same time tomorrow ;) ::

There was a flurry of emojis and comments from the stream users. Ranging from good wishes to graphic propositions. None of it phased him anymore; as a medical student, he'd found it occasionally informative.

Chase was about to end the stream when a familiar account name flashed up on the screen.

Kyanite.

One of the rarest silicate minerals found on the

mining planet, the username sat between mysterious and pompous.

As with most patrons on the live streams, there was no picture and very little information in his profile. Which, of course, Chase had checked after the first few times they'd interacted. He was sure most were ex-prospectors from core planets, stuck here just like he was, for now. But this one gave off a completely different vibe to all the others, so he hadn't been surprised to discover that he was a resettled centaurian, all the way from Proxima Centauri b – colloquially shortened to "B" – to this shit hole.

Relocating to a human prospector colony was strange enough. The few centaurians stood out amongst the smooth-skinned humans, their soft scales and bald heads always slightly taller than those around them. Chase wasn't sure why any of them would want to live in such a place and so far from their own kind. Very intriguing.

:: Beautiful as always, sweet boy ::

The words appeared followed, as Chase expected, by a little ping and a notification in the top corner of the screen.

-- Kyanite has requested a private audience. Accept? --

-- Yes/No --

Chase wanted to pretend that he hesitated before he said, "Screen, end stream, and connect to Kyanite."

The stream feed went dead and then a moment later was replaced with a messaging screen, text only as Chase preferred, usually. For most people.

But with Kyanite, he made an exception and pressed the toggle in the top corner, switching it from text only to a video connection.

"There is a meteor shower above my home this evening, and whilst I am sure it is a beautiful sight, your beauty eclipses it." The centaurian crooned the words as soon as his image appeared.

Chase knew well enough that centaurians could be manipulative, but something about Kyanite never made him doubt his words or his clear adoration. There was nothing for him to gain by his flirtations, nothing that he certainly couldn't buy with Chase or any other streamers. But it was Chase he seemed to have affection for.

Chase sucked in a breath and let it out as his heart thumped. It was difficult to pretend the feeling wasn't mutual. As much as he tried to keep his distance from his audience, Kyanite had certainly gotten under his skin.

It had started with little notes when Chase hadn't initially accepted a private audience months ago. He never did with anyone. He was happy with just his one-way shows. He would take on board some suggestions of what people might like to see the next time, but this way, it was all on him, and he liked having that control. He had no plans to open a private chat and have someone dictate what they wanted him to do for their pleasure.

And yet he couldn't ignore the little throb in his cock at the thought of letting Kyanite do just that.

Kyanite's first message stood out, unlike the dick pics and the proposals he often received in his notes. It was first an apology for having requested the private audience, realising it was something Chase wasn't comfortable with. Kyanite had then waxed poetic about Chase's beauty and ingenuity before saying that he hoped Chase would allow him to send more messages in the future. If he'd ignored it, perhaps Kyanite would never have replied again. And indeed, he didn't for the week that Chase *had* ignored it.

In the end, Chase replied *:: Go ahead ::*

And from there, the conversations began.

Chase was still cagey, not wanting to give anything away that might make his life difficult; he gave only basic replies to questions if anything. And most of the time, the messages required no response. They simply made him smile, and he found he'd started to look forward to them dropping into his inbox once or twice a week.

He knew he should be cautious, but there was surely nothing wrong with such a small amount of contact, even if he had started to anticipate them with a light feeling in his chest. And it wasn't lost on him that their discussions hinted that should Chase ever want to find himself a lover, it should be someone who approved of how he made money and supported his ventures. It felt like their conversations were more than a patron and a camboy. It felt like they were friends, flirtatious friends. A friend to whom Chase started to give private shows.

"Flattery will get you nowhere," Chase grinned, aware that his cheeks were flush.

"I simply express the truth as I see it."

Chase looked away but saw the grin out of the

corner of his eye; Kyanite was always amused by the effect he had.

"I have sent you a gift, my sweet boy. It is waiting with your postal service." Kyanite purred.

"Oh, you don't need to get me gifts," Chase protested, though making a note to get the postal service to release it to him. That way, he needn't give out his address to strangers.

"I think you'll find it's a gift more so for myself. If you are willing to indulge me in a private show tomorrow evening? After your usual stream, of course."

"Yes," Chase replied, breathless and blushing. He couldn't hide how much he enjoyed doing private shows for Kyanite.

Within minutes, as usual, a large sum of credits appeared in his account with the note *:: I look forward to it ::*

Chase spent a few minutes getting everything ready, tidying his spartan room so that there was nothing viewable that was even remotely personal. Just his bed and plain blankets, the bedside drawers with the top drawer open and toys already hanging out of it ready.

Chase took a breath and lay down on the bed.

There was a rumble outside, and the lights flickered momentarily. He had known the electrical storm was coming in, and they sometimes got bad on this side of the planet, so he was logging on a little earlier than usual just in case the power went out.

He hadn't had as much prep time to work himself up to it as he liked. It was always more manageable if he got himself worked up a little first, so he lay back and started to stroke his cock, feeling the wetness gather beneath it. It wasn't until he let out a quiet but desperate moan that he realised he was thinking of Kyanite. His soft, deep voice cooed honeyed words.

Chase was achingly hard and wet by the time he tapped his tablet and brought the Screen to life. His stream went live, and immediately his room was filled with the sounds of little pings as people joined the stream. Little hearts flitted up the side, and comments scrolled by, eager and waiting for him to fuck himself for them.

Chase bit down on his lower lip, turning his body so they could see him rummaging in the drawer as though deliberating on what toy to use, though he had already decided after picking up the gift from Kyanite. To add to the tease, he looked back over his shoulder, wide eyes at the cam, "There are just so many to choose from."

It was good to draw out the beginning; it allowed more people to drop in and encouraged more credit drops. Plus, the image capture for the stream was taken at one-minute intervals, so he was presenting a nice little promo right now to reel people in before he got down to business.

"Maybe this one," Chase made the most innocent, doe-eyed expression possible as he rolled back to the pillows and placed the dildo on his lap.

"But… it's so big."

Pings sounded, and the credits were dropping in.

"In my ass?"

More pings affirmed the decision.

The dildo he had chosen was one he found particularly favourable for anal. It was long and had a thick girth but started thin and tapered. It was somewhat like a tentacle in appearance and reasonably malleable—a great way to open his ass up.

"Are you sure?" He asked the audience, "It might hurt…"

The credit pings became a cacophony of encouragement. Chase blinked innocently and then took the lube from the drawer, pooling a good amount into his cupped hand, before working it up and down the dildo sitting erect between his legs.

He made those encouraging, sweet moans as he did so, and there was another flurry of credits, of new joiners, and then more credits.

The storm rumbling closer, lightning flashes of brightness in the mood lighting of his room, made the whole scene completely perfect. It had definitely been the right, monstrous choice of toy.

With wide, blinking eyes, Chase pulled the dildo back and ran the tip over his t-cock, legs falling open to give the audience the view they paid for.

Chase made a show of the pleasure, the room reverberating with the sound of credits as he teased his wet front hole before sliding it back towards his asshole.

He moved onto his knees, facing the camera, and then moaned as he slid the toy inside.

"Oh god…" He moaned, knowing more vocalising always gained him more credits.

And yes, more dropped in as he rode the dildo, panting, grunting, and muttering how it was *so* good.

And it was. It really was.

Which Chase had to admit was beyond the toy. He had to admit that he was thinking about the toy Kyanite had sent, one based on centaurian anatomy, which he'd be taking to their private show shortly.

He slipped his fingers down to his front hole, gathering up some of the wetness there before sliding them up over his cock and beginning to wank himself with the two fingers. He orchestrated a tried and tested move to flip himself around so that his ass was facing the camera.

Although his patrons could no longer see his fingers, they saw the movement of his arm and now had a close-up view of the dildo going in and out of his ass.

"It's so big!" Chase groaned.

ping ping ping

"I'm going to come, nhhghhh."

ping ping ping ping ping

"Imagine it's your cock in my ass, baby." He told the audience as he clenched. There were more pings as he flexed his hole around the dildo, giving them the best possible angle.

"Nnnnnggg, I'm so full!" Chase groaned.

ping ping ping ping ping

"Gonna—"

ping ping ping ping ping ping ping ping ping ping

"Ughhhhnnnfffff," Chase cried out and came, the pings ringing in his ears. He breathed heavily for a few moments before falling forward and carefully sliding the dildo out of him. When he flopped down on the bed, there were more pings, almost like applause, and then they began to peter off as usual.

Still panting, Chase pulled himself over to the screen and smiled his dopey, blissed-out grin. "Thanks, everyone. Same time tomorrow."

He watched the steady stream of aroused, appreciative and explicit messages scroll up the feed, his eyes catching on one.

:: My beautiful boy ::

Chase felt his cheeks heat and gave a little wave before ending the stream. And then he paused.

He felt like he was on the precipice of something. Kyanite had sent him small gifts before. Chocolates, some centaurian sweet delicacies, and a small butt plug once. But this gift, a toy that he evidently wanted Chase to use during their private call, felt like it carried some other proposition or expectation with it.

Chase took in a deep breath. He wanted to show Kyanite that he could find pleasure with a centaurian. And, yes, he did want to clarify that there was one centaurian in particular that he wanted to know intimately.

"Screen, connect to Kyanite."

Immediately he was in the private room and flipping the toggle over to video mode. Kyanite was smiling at him fondly.

"I enjoyed that a great deal," the centaurian purred.

Chase blushed, "I hate that centaurians are cold-blooded. I can never tell if you're flustered or not."

"My dear boy, I can assure you that your performance very, very deeply moves me."

Chase grinned and lay back on the bed again, relaxing naked under Kyanite's gaze as they smiled at each other. He never felt this comfortable with anyone else. The stream was okay because it wasn't a real connection, just a faceless audience. But in person, he was more cautious with lovers and about what they wanted from him or his body. He felt safe and warm with Kyanite as he laid himself bare for the man.

Damn, he really did like him. And it wasn't just the flattery or the fact that he found him sexually attractive. He just... he was a gentleman, the sort that Chase never hoped to meet. He was on a planet of economic collapse and was engaging in sex work not only to get through school but because he enjoyed it. Not the sort of man a *gentleman* should be interested in. All the more intriguing that they are different species.

"You never touch yourself, do you," Chase remarked, "when you watch my shows. I'm sure I could tell if you were flustered then."

"I do not," Kyanite confirmed, "it seems ungentlemanly."

Chase laughed at the coincidental word choice, stroking a hand idly down his ribs.

"Then why do you watch at all?"

"I enjoy beautiful things. And, I will admit, since finding your stream, I have ceased seeking any others. When you come, it is more beautiful than sunset on B."

Chase blushed but didn't speak further. Instead, he reached over the side of the bed and picked up the present he had been sent.

"I want to know what you feel like," Chase said, grabbing the lube and slicking the toy. It was a dildo in the shape of centaurian anatomy. Two penes, one ever so slightly smaller and curved than the other. And while they would usually twist together to enter a centaurian female's front hole, Chase had already given away what he planned to do in his stream.

Gently, as he lubed the shafts, he pulled the malleable material apart so that the two cocks were free of each other.

"Is this how you'd fuck me?" Chase asked, meaning it. Not dirty talk this time to get the cash rolling in, but because he actually wanted to know. "It's how I imagine you fucking me."

There was the slightest sound from Kyanite's throat, but his demeanour did not change as he watched Chase spread his legs and slowly sink the dildo into both his holes.

He had to mould them slightly as he went, curving them so they fit him perfectly, but Chase could hardly breathe by the time they were completely inside him.

"So good, you feel so good," Chase muttered as he slid the dildo almost all the way out before steadily pushing it back in. He repeated this a few times, his body shuddering every time he bottomed out. "Kyanite…" Chase whispered his name and continued to fuck himself, eyes meeting the centaurian's as he watched stoically.

"Want to wrap my legs around you and pull you deep. Want you to fuck me so hard." Chase muttered the words as he pumped the dildo in and out. "Hmm, Kyanite…" Chase closed his eyes, blissed out at the sensation of being so full.

"Blin."

Chase's eyes sprang open, and he saw the determination in the centaurian's expression. It was clear, for once, how close he was to losing control.

"My name is Blin," he said, eyes boring into Chase.

"Blin," Chase gasped, fucking himself deeper and faster, "I want you inside me."

Chase forced himself to keep his eyes open as he writhed and panted. His whole body was flushed, and he moved one hand to pinch a nipple, noting how Blin's eyes flicked to the movement.

"Do you want me to come, Blin? Come all over your cocks with your name on my lips?" Chase pushed, so close already, but he ran the hand down from his chest to his cock and teased at it.

Chase didn't miss the way Blin's jaw clenched, and then, instead of responding verbally, he gave a curt nod.

Chase moaned and closed his eyes, spreading his legs as wide as he could as he continued to fuck himself with the dildo and stroke his cock in time with the thrusts.

"Blin, Blin." He gasped, "oh… MMm… nnhghhh… Blin…" He released a few more throaty sounds before he came, squirting all over his hand and dildo. He clenched tight around the cocks inside him, which only made his climax all the stronger.

And he certainly didn't miss the sound coming from the other side of the Screen. He opened his eyes to see nothing but a dark and dangerous desire in the centaurian's eyes as he let out a hum of pleasure.

"My beautiful boy, you took me so well." Blin cooed as Chase sank back onto the bed, still trembling through his orgasm.

After trying to level his breathing, Chase looked at Blin, knowing his desire was mirrored there.

"I want to take you, Blin. I want you inside me. For real." Chase breathed out the words before he could hold them back.

Blin's mouth curved into a grin, "And perhaps next time I am in your region, that can be arranged. But, I would want to do the gentlemanly thing and take you to dinner first if that is acceptable." It wasn't a question, but Chase understood his meaning. He wouldn't want to treat him as a whore but as a date, as a lover. "And I can't promise, once I have had you, that I could live without having you again and again."

Chase let out a long, sated sigh and nodded. His intrigue was piqued all the more. They were strange people in this place, aliens in their own ways. There was a comfort in that Chase hadn't realised he wanted or needed.

"I would like that very much," Chase replied with a sigh, his holes clenching again just at the thought of being together in person. "Can we do this again tomorrow night?" Chase asked before adding quickly, "I don't mean for you to pay. I mean—"

"For me to watch you as a lover might," Blin spoke coolly, amusement playing across his lips.

"Yes," Chase replied breathlessly, "but this time... I, um... I want to see you too, like tonight but with you... I want to see the pleasure I know you'll take once this call ends."

Blin's smile grew, "indeed? Well, in that case, I better prepare to put on quite a show for you, my beautiful boy."

They grinned stupidly at each other before Chase finally nodded and said, "Okay then. Same time tomorrow."

Fools and their Money

Kurt finds the perfect way to make money.

Content Notes: Trans man/cis male android.
Modelling, sex work, android sex, pornographic photography, live sex stream.
Anatomical References: PIV penetration.
Reference to top surgery.

"That's it, Kurt. Moan for me." The voice was rich and deep, tinged with a slightly metallic echo.

And Kurt did. He moaned and twisted his body under the android, turned on by the sound of escaping air as its joints moved.

Kurt had only intended to do this once. There was much money to be made in android smut, a very specialised clientele who would pay good money. The models could make some serious cash, and the photographers were all androids, so their money went to their agency and kept them in oil and batteries.

Being with an android might be taboo to many, but Kurt liked that it was utterly devoid of emotional connection and had no medical risks. And for the clientele, the appeal was in the camera lens eyes, giving the photo recipients the sense of being part of the act.

Somewhere out there, a whole bunch of people were jerking off over his tight little body, getting pounded by the same android he always requested.

The one that he kept coming back for. The one that seemed to like him back, even though he knew that couldn't be the case.

In truth, Kurt had planned to join the military. There was okay money in it, and they'd pay for him to get his medical procedures like he wanted. Something that otherwise wasn't going to happen. Especially as he had to help support his family since his dad left.

He could have just done it the once and left it at that – enough to set his mum up until he could send money back from deployment. But that hadn't happened.

Kurt enjoyed it, and what's more, he particularly enjoyed Antron Twelve. After years of never feeling entirely comfortable being naked around people, years of being self-conscious and fumbling in the dark, he'd met someone – something – which made him feel comfortable and acceptable in his skin.

Kurt knew it wasn't real, but he couldn't stop.

It wasn't like Antron felt anything for him; he couldn't. But that didn't matter; Kurt needed him all the same.

That first time, in the end, he had paid for his top surgery, and subsequent times had helped him build a fanbase, selling first photos and then videos of his time with Antron – all through Antron's beautiful pale grey eyes.

This was it, Kurt realised. This was all he

needed. A job he loved that more than paid the bills. And he did so love being fucked by Antron.

Kurt gasped, "There, please! Fuck me right there."

He looked adoringly up at the android. Besides the slight green tinge to his skin, Antron could pass as a human. He was top of the line and, at least to Kurt's mind, looked like some military general, which made the experience all the hotter for Kurt, who really did have a thing for uniforms. A buff older man that looked like he might be able to crush him as soon as look at him? That was precisely what Kurt wanted, and he'd found him in Antron.

"Mhmm, such a good boy," Antron replied, running his hands up Kurt's flanks and then to his hard nipples, tweaking them as Kurt heard a series of little clicks as Antron took photos even as the scene was live-streamed to Kurt's channel. He encouraged Kurt to writhe and moan, delivering as much pleasure as possible to get the best from him.

Antron's grunt sounded slightly mechanical as he pushed deep into Kurt, and multiple clicks went off. He photographed Kurt's angelic and ecstasy-filled expression as pleasure blossomed. He photographed Kurt's cock coming untouched.

Kurt knew part of his appeal was being trans. He knew there were many subscribers there for that reason alone. But he didn't let it bother him, deciding early on that if the fools wanted to fetishise or objectify him, the least they could do was pay handsomely for it. And as his mother always said, a fool and their money were easily parted.

So, for now, he wouldn't think about the future and the longevity of this. Perhaps he'd start setting money aside to buy Antron once his money-making days were over?

But he didn't need to think about that for now, not as he lay on his back being photographed by the android fucking him through his climax. He just had to marvel that making so much money doing something he utterly loved was unbelievable.

Connect

Remy makes an unexpected connection.

Content Notes: Trans man/non-binary android.
Prejudice and bigotry (against androids), violence,
bigoted attack (on an android), self-hatred, finger
fucking (front hole), virginity, loss of virginity,
reference to porn watching, oral sex on a trans man,
penetrative sex (front hole), android spunk.
Anatomical References: PIV penetration. Packer
wearing. Cock, dick and t-cock, and vague terms:
hard, wet, hole, juices and entrance used for trans
male genitalia. Reference to gender incongruence
and genital swapping/changing (on an android).

"I've had just about enough of this shit." Remy
cursed, then muttered, "Fucking tin can."

He turned from the android and started stalking
down the hallway away from the ambulance bay.
He really was done with this shit. He never asked to
be assigned a fucking robot, though with each crew
eventually being assigned one, it has only been a
matter of time.

Almost human was the selling point. Human
enough to have something near a bedside manner
but with the diagnostic speed of a computer. They
would replace them all in the end, until every job

was just a robot, Remy was sure. Especially now that they had actual rights. *Sentient* rights.

Remy paid lip service to the whole thing, like everyone did. He made like he was playing nice and adjusting to his new *colleague*. That he wasn't as intolerant of androids as he really was, now that they were, apparently, actual people. But the fact was, he had always disliked them, and nothing was going to change that overnight. And he wasn't sure he wanted it to.

And now he had this new fucking partner who tested his prejudice daily.

An android that had chosen to become a paramedic now that they had the right to choose careers.

He continued to storm down the hallway, heading for the double doors to the break room, but he could hear P-Med87 following closely behind him.

What was the fucking point of having one of these damn machines as a paramedic if they still lost the patient?

And in truth, that was where his anger lay today. All this effort he had to put in not to get written up by his boss, and what was even the point?

And P-Med87? He wasn't like the rest of them, which maybe made Remy even more uneasy. The earlier models? They hadn't looked human. They had been what they were supposed to be – robotic assistants in the field. These newer ones had freaked Remy out *before* they gained sentience.

Since that very first day, P-Med87 had been cold and unfriendly. As hostile and terse with Remy as

Remy had been to the tin can. And that was terrifying because it meant they really were sentient if they didn't have to be chirpy and smiling all the time, like the early models.

"Specialist," P-Med87 called out to him, but Remy kept walking. He just needed one day not to end in a fucking argument with this walking computer. "Specialist Okoye, please halt."

Remy clenched his jaw as he turned on his heel, stopping in front of the android as requested. He wasn't about to get written up because of this asshole.

"My shift is over. So is yours. Go plug yourself into a power socket or whatever the hell you do."

"We need to talk about what happened," the words were firm, and Remy heard the annoyance there.

And, the thing was, P-Med87 might be right.

They had lost a patient. It happened, and in this case, no other outcome was possible. The injuries were too extensive; the situation would have been the same even if they'd arrived sooner. It still hurt. Every death did.

And with his old partner, Remy would have gone to the bar and had a couple of drinks. Both to soften life around the edges a little and as a fuck you to God. And occasionally, whilst there, he'd pick up someone and go home with them, a reminder to live life to the fullest.

The truth was, it was easier and made him feel a little better to blame P-Med87.

He wasn't about to go to a bar with a robot.

Six Months Later

"Good work, Specialist." Pasha smiled as he raised his empty glass. They'd attended a large incident earlier that day for which Remy had ended up as the incident commander. It wasn't the first time, and Remy knew he was good at it. If he kept going like this, promotion was on the cards.

Then, he could leave P-Med87 behind. Or Pasha, as he had decided to be called.

He could take a command position and not have to worry about androids. This was, of course, not true; in command, he'd have many answerable to him, but he wouldn't have to work side by side with them like he had to with Pasha.

He raised his glass, this one with actual alcohol, and downed it.

The sooner he could get away from Pasha, the better.

"Thanks." Remy made his usual grunt, never entirely covering the discomfort he felt. Not at the easy way they conversed now, but the fact that he enjoyed it. That he fucking appreciated it and didn't want ever to admit that to anyone, least of all the tin can in front of him.

He had increasingly enjoyed the android's company since the first time they'd gone to the bar together after a rough shift. It was getting more difficult every day to hold onto the prejudice he felt, harder to not see Pasha as a person. As a friend.

"I will remain humble about my own efforts on the case." Pasha continued, and Remy had to look at him to work out if he was serious. The android smirked, and then Remy understood he was joking, teasing, in that weird way he had.

Remy let out a chuckle before he could help himself and relaxed on the barstool.

Pasha was still cold at work, but part of that was concentration, Remy had realised. And the rest had been him just giving Remy a taste of his own medicine. More and more, Remy thought that maybe he'd deserved that.

"I never thought I'd say this, but you're not so bad, Pasha. As a paramedic." He admitted with a smile of his own. Damn, he'd had way too much to drink – actually complimenting this bucket of bolts.

The android looked taken aback, cocking his head and raising a brow. "You've never called me that before."

"What? Pasha? Sure I have," Remy dismissed with a wave of his hand, though now he thought about it, maybe Pasha was right. It was the name the android had chosen to go by, the one everyone at work now called him. The one he'd selected amongst the millions of names out there for reasons locked away in that whirling brain box.

Remy shook off the unwelcome sense of understanding.

"No," Pasha replied with a smile and a slight shake of his head. "Not once, *Specialist*."

That seemed odd. How had he not said it before? P-Med87 had been going by Pasha since a few weeks on the job.

"What do I call you then?" At that, Pasha raised his eyebrows, and Remy chuckled and waved him off, "Yeah, okay, Tin Can."

When the laughter subsided, Pasha stood up. "I should go now, Specialist. And you should probably go home and sleep. This has been an exhausting day."

Remy drank the last of his pint even as he waved Pasha off.

The Android rolled his eyes and then walked to the exit.

The day *had* been exhausting, and as with all days like this, Remy was caught between one more drink and sleeping. Remy looked back to the bar and sat alone now; he wasn't sure he was bothered about another pint.

He didn't usually care much about drinking alone, but he had to admit Pasha leaving seemed to have taken the fun out of it. He waved the server off, grabbed his jacket, and headed to the door.

"Fucking piece of shit!" Remy heard the commotion as soon as he stepped outside of the bar. No one was on the street, but then more shouting and the sound of trash cans being thrown about directed his attention to the alley next to the bar. "I got laid off because of pricks like you."

There was a sound of flesh connecting, the unmistakable sound of a fist connecting with a face, but with that strange flat noise that came with hitting an android. Remy ran towards the sound, turning the corner to expect to break up a fight. He wasn't expecting the three men holding Pasha against the wall and beating the ever-loving shit out of him.

"Hey!" Remy shouted, pulling his phone out and tapping the screen to show the direct line to the

Services Station they were based out of. He held up his phone so the dickheads could see it, one tap and he was calling directly to the nearest police, fire and paramedic station. "It's been a long night, fellas. I don't want to have to deal with the paperwork for this, and I know the cops won't want to either. So, hows about you let the android go? Huh? You know it's a felony now, not just property damage. You'll be brought in for assault."

That seemed to get a rise from them, but none moved as they jeered at him. Remy continued to advance, his thumb hovering over the green *Connect* dot.

"Don't make me ask again."

Grumbling, they let go of Pasha so that the android hit the ground, and all started backing away.

"Don't worry, Specialist," Pasha said, calm and collected as ever. "I have already called for backup."

The moment the words left his mouth, sirens closed in on them, and the men scattered. A car pulled up at the top of the alley, and officers from their Services Station crowded in.

"That way, fellas," Remy waved toward the running perps.

"I'll need to give a statement," Pasha noted as Remy went to him and set him on his feet, ensuring he was steady.

"Just access the file number and download your—"

Pasha gave him a withering look like he didn't need to be told what to do. Which, of course, he didn't. His eyes glazed over momentarily, the pupils agitating too fast to see as the information was communicated back to the station.

"Done," Pasha replied a moment later. "I should go now."

"Wait, you need to get checked over. Are you okay?" Remy asked, frowning as Pasha tried to walk past him.

"I am uninjured, Remy. There is no need for concern." Pasha replied coolly, a slight smirk on his face.

Remy sucked in a breath at the words—the tone. Pasha had a way of saying his name that made Remy's insides feel weird, but it wasn't just that. He hadn't been prepared for the relief he felt at hearing Pasha was alright.

Pasha frowned and cocked his head, "Are *you* alright?"

"I'm fine. It's nothing," Remy grunted, then winced at sounding like a brat. He shook his head, trying to hide his reaction.

"Were you injured, Specialist?" Pasha asked. "You appear to be in distress—"

"I'm fine," Remy ground out through his teeth, then turned and stalked down the alley.

"Specialist!" Pasha called out after him, and then he could hear the android's footfall behind him. "Remy."

Pasha took hold of Remy's arm and pulled him to stop and turn.

"What?" Remy snapped.

Pasha released his arm and blinked, taken aback.

"I'll drive you home," Pasha said coolly, to which Remy grunted and consented, knowing that he really should get a taxi as he had planned but couldn't quite bring himself to.

Remy didn't speak as they drove back to his apartment. Too concerned about what he might say if he opened his mouth.

He hated to admit it but seeing Pasha like that had shaken him up.

How many fucking times had he watched androids beaten up, pulled apart, shot? How many times had he not cared? He hadn't been the most tolerant of people when it came to androids.

But maybe Pasha had begun to change his opinion.

Not just Pasha. Maybe the other P-Meds too? It was hard to deny their sentience when it was right before him. Even if he hadn't wanted to accept it and it didn't like them, they had minds of their own.

And if they were sentient, then his hatred for them was fucked up. Wasn't it? How could he hate another living thing and not be the bad guy? And that shit was something he knew well. The world still wasn't accepting of all kinds of people, and he'd experienced that first-hand in his youth. It should have made him more empathetic, but it didn't; it hardened him. And the androids had been on the blunt end of that hardness that now seemed misdirected.

Pasha had really started to change his mind about how he perceived them.

He had known this droid from the day he'd arrived at the station. He'd been there as he'd learned and grown and applied everything that had come before being a paramedic to the person he was now.

Remy's partner. His friend.

Remy swallowed.

"Do you need assistance getting into the apartment?" Pasha asked, concern in his tone.

Remy had automatically intended to say no. He'd have said no to anyone, saving face and maintaining his hard-won machismo. But he didn't want to say goodbye to Pasha yet. And he tried to hate feeling that way. He wanted to hate Pasha for the things he brought out in him.

He'd always been an asshole, and he knew that. But it went deeper than that. He was guarded and wary and never let anyone close. Much less a damn tin can.

"Yeah, sure," Remy grunted, wanting to sound put out even as his heart thundered in his chest. Remy opened the car door and got out.

Pasha was behind him, following close as though ready to catch him. As though Remy had been the one attacked or as if he had had too much to drink. Maybe he had.

When they entered the apartment, Remy threw his keys onto the sideboard as usual, leaving Pasha to close the door. He continued as though this were an ordinary evening, not least because there was something weird about having Pasha in his space at that moment.

Pasha had never been to his apartment before. It changed the dynamic, and Remy didn't feel as secure in his own space as usual. In fact, instead of feeling like he was on home ground, Remy felt vulnerable.

He was stiff and felt awkward, his back to Pasha.

"Remy, what is it?" Pasha asked softly, at which Remy tensed.

His automatic reaction was always to be on the defensive. He always had been, especially when confronted with his own feelings. And Remy wasn't obtuse enough not to recognise how he felt now because of what had happened. Seeing Pasha under threat and the fear that rolled over him had thrown him off balance.

Whether Pasha realised it or not, it had thrown their dynamic off, and Remy wasn't comfortable with that because he didn't want to acknowledge it.

"You could have fucking died," Remy growled his accusation, not turning.

"Androids don't d—"

"Okay!" Remy threw up his hands as he turned, facing Pasha. He balled his fists, shaking with anger that he knew was misplaced. "I get it. But you're a person now, right? You could have been torn apart and not repairable and—"

Remy ran out of steam, still shaking.

"That isn't it. Tell me, Remy. Why are you really angry?"

"Because I want you to take it seriously," Remy growled, unable to hold the words back as he stalked to Pasha, pointing a finger in his face. "You need to give a shit if you get injured or killed. You *affect* people."

Pasha opened his mouth to speak, but Remy was too far gone, too riled up. Too full of whatever this was coursing through him. Rage? Passion? Whatever it was, it wanted to explode out of his body.

He slammed into Pasha, nearly knocking him off his feet, and grabbed the back of his neck. He met Pasha's eyes for just a moment; certain he could see *something* there before he forced their mouths together in a heated kiss that was very quickly not one-sided.

Remy groaned as Pasha's hands came up to cup his face, kissing him back almost brutally until Remy was out of breath and had to pull back. Not just pulling back, he moved his hands to Pasha's chest and pushed the android away as hard as he could, shaking his head.

How could he have just done that? He was so fucking hard and wet because of a fucking android. His face burned red, and he tried to crush the feelings that he'd been trying to ignore for weeks. Pasha was like him in some ways. Different. Not the norm that people expected, but unlike Remy, Pasha didn't try to fit in. He hadn't turned into an angry, nasty piece of shit like Remy had. And that was a lot to process.

"Get out," Remy shouted, at which Pasha didn't flinch or move.

"Remy, whatever this is—" Pasha started calmly.

"Please, get out," Remy growled, looking down at his once more balled fists, his voice quietly shaking with anger. At himself, not Pasha. For feeling this way at all.

Saw another fucking misfit and latched onto them? He wasn't a fucking kid any more, finding the other kids who were outsiders too. And then fucking them over when he realised he could work out, build up strength and muscle and ditch the nerds for bullies like he'd become.

Fuck, he hated himself.

He hated himself so much that his chest hurt. It was hard to breathe, and his eyes felt wet.

When Pasha tentatively reached for one of his hands, Remy didn't pull away. But he didn't unclench his fist as Pasha stroked his fingers over his balled hand.

Despite the initial coolness, as the contact continued, Pasha felt so warm, so real. Remy wasn't sure he'd expected Pasha to feel like that. So different but so human at the same time.

He wasn't sure if that made this better or worse.

"You were worried about me," Pasha stated.

Remy clenched his jaw and shook his head.

"You're fighting yourself," Pasha observed, and Remy was hard pressed to deny it. "You don't want to care for me. Your heart is racing. It seems that you are—" Pasha had the good grace to stop there, not point out that he could sense the reaction of Remy's body, his arousal.

Everything inside him was roiling. He wanted Pasha. He fucking wanted him and hated that he did.

Yes, partly because he was an android, but it wasn't just that. Remy never wanted anyone, always kept everyone at arm's length, his walls up. And now this android was breaking through that? Fuck no.

And yet when Remy moved his hand to push Pasha away again, he found his fingers unfurling and then their fingers interlinked. He swallowed as he looked at their joined hands.

"What is it, Remy? What's holding you back?" Pasha asked calmly, but it just angered Remy over again. "I would be receptive."

"No, I—" He cut himself off, unsure what he was even going to say. It was so hard to ignore all this with Pasha so close. With their fingers linked together like fucking lovers.

Remy sucked in a breath as Pasha reached forward with his other hand and cupped his face again, stroking his thumb over Remy's stubble.

"I feel this thing too," Pasha said, "Whatever it is, these sensations, these *feelings*."

"Fuck." Remy pulled away completely, stalking back and forth in the room. This was all too fucking much.

"Please, what is it, Remy?" Pasha asked gently. A slight edge of insistence to his voice made Remy angry.

"I— I don't let people close," Remy muttered as he paced. A statement more than anything, as though this would halt everything in their tracks.

"You fear rejection," Pasha replied, stating it as a fact. "I have known you long enough, Remy, to understand the patterns of your behaviour. The way you treat people. Your lack of any close friends. Except me. Because you feel the same way I do and want to let me close."

Remy tightened his jaw.

"You should go," He insisted again, backing up against the wall as Pasha approached him.

"Or should I stay?" Pasha asked, the slight edge of a threat. Which was precisely what Remy needed, as he was sure the android knew. To have the decision taken out of his hands.

"Do you want me to decide for you?" Pasha asked, and Remy had barely given a slight nod before he found himself pressed against the wall. "Is that what you want, Remy?"

"Fuck, yes." Remy spat the words, almost angry. At Pasha? At himself for not being able to maintain control? He wasn't sure. He just knew he didn't want to be in control anymore; he just wanted to let everything happen.

"I'll stay," Pasha replied.

With a grunt that was so very human, Pasha pressed an arm across Remy's chest, holding him there as he slid the other hand down to Remy's jeans. The android undid Remy's belt and fly with speed and precision without having to even look down.

It left Remy breathless and shaking.

He should stop this; he knew he should. But he wanted it so fucking bad, too bad even to consider the reality of what was about to happen.

"Fuck," Was all he managed to say before Pasha's hand was down the front of his trousers and taking hold of his packer. He squeezed it and pushed it against Remy's actual cock, grinding it against him. "Oh fuck!"

Pasha hummed, a flicker of something in his eyes. A recognition and adjustment. He hadn't known that Remy was trans; that seemed clear, but apparently, neither did he care.

"This is okay, Remy. You know that, don't you?" Pasha damn near whispered the words in his ear. His tone was reassuring as he gently fondled the packer with explicit knowledge of what it was and why it was there.

Remy's heavy panting illustrated that Pasha didn't need to draw breath, but even so, he seemed far from calm. Gone was the emotionless, logical machine. Now, there were feelings, desires.

"I've wanted this for a long time," Pasha growled, and it was almost enough to make Remy whimper, but he held it back. "I want you, Remy. Just as you are."

"Damn it, just…" Remy growled, wanting more and grinding against Pasha's hand. "Touch me. Get rid of the packer."

With a hum, Pasha did as bid, pulled the packer out, and dropped it on the floor with a soft thud before returning his hand. He slid it slowly into Remy's boxers as Remy moaned.

He was so wet that there was no resistance to the slightly cool flesh as it met his heated centre.

Remy let out a groan as Pasha easily pushed two fingers slowly inside of him. The hotter Remy felt, the cooler Pasha seemed, and it felt so fucking good. He could feel every slide and flex as he spread his legs enough for Pasha to start slowly fucking him with his fingers.

"Oh fuck." Remy muttered, taking hold of Pasha's shoulders and holding tight.

"Bedroom?" Pasha asked, a breathless quality there that Remy knew was an affectation, but one Pasha had desired to perform anyway.

"Y–yeah," Remy panted.

He whined as Pasha withdrew his fingers but then led the way to the bedroom, shaking with anticipation.

Their entrance to the bedroom couldn't have been more different. Pasha slowly and deliberately removed his clothes as he watched Remy intently. Whilst Remy frantically shed his clothes, pulling them so firmly that it was a wonder nothing ripped.

"How do you want me?" Pasha asked softly as Remy climbed onto the bed.

"Fuck," Remy froze, his gaze roaming over Pasha's slowly revealed form.

He looked fucking beautiful, and Remy hadn't wholly expected that. He'd expected some fake form of perfection, maybe something too perfect. But that wasn't the case; Pasha looked real, his athletic proportions and light brown skin, everything right down to his happy trail and neatly trimmed pubes, and his impressive cock.

Not grossly huge, not too small. A perfect size and pleasing shape. It seemed almost seamlessly attached but for a thin scar-like circle around his crotch area, denoting it as interchangeable.

Remy whined when Pasha removed the last of his clothes and stroked his cock.

"I—I thought…" Remy started, interrupted by Pasha's chuckle.

"We don't come with appendages?" Pasha smiled softly as he continued to stroke himself, clearly finding it pleasurable as his cock reacted as any would, getting harder and harder in his hand. "Not as standard, unless a sex model. Many of us opted to acquire some sort of genitalia after gaining sentience."

"I like it," Remy gasped, pulling himself backwards on the bed until he rested against the headboard. He spread his legs a little, starting to stoke his t-cock.

Pasha's smile quirked slightly, and Remy wondered if androids could blush.

"I acquired this one recently. I have others. Some male, some female. Some are customised, in between." Pasha told him as he began moving steadily forward toward the bed. Too soft to be called stalking, but a determination there nonetheless.

"Do all androids do that?" Remy asked, curiosity piqued at the idea of what Pasha was suggesting.

"Have multiple genitalia? Yes. In fact, if we had to describe it in human terms, most androids would identify as non-binary."

Remy frowned, "Because you can change genitals?"

"No," Pasha shook his head, "because of how we feel inside, how *I* feel. I change my genitals because of how I feel, not vice versa. Our outer surface is only what has been assigned to us, after all. Inside, I don't feel male or female, or sometimes I feel both. But I was made to look male. And whilst I am happy to present as male, it's not always how I feel." Pasha spoke as he crawled up the bed and held himself over Remy.

Remy looked directly into Pasha's deep brown eyes, taking in every word. He had hated androids for not being human, and now he'd discovered that he likely had more in common with them than half the humans he knew. Their gender had been assigned, too; it had never occurred to him that they might find it incongruent.

"Fuck," Remy shook his head.

"Perhaps we can explore my genitalia collection together sometime."

Remy groaned, thinking about all the possibilities.

"I have... I have a few cocks." Remy panted as pumped his cock between his fingers, "Love to fuck you with one of them one day. Maybe we can compare." He grinned.

Pasha returned the grin, hovering over him.

"Is that what you want? To fuck me? I'd let you..."

"Fuck," Remy gasped, sliding his fingers down to tease at his wet entrance. "Sounds fucking great, but not this time. I want you inside me tonight. Fuck, want you real bad."

Pasha hummed his interest and lowered himself back down Remy's body, "I've never been with anyone before." He muttered, his breath whispering cold over Remy's abdomen. "But I have downloaded many instructions."

"Into your brain?"

"No," Pasha chuckled, causing Remy to shiver at the sensation of his breath between his legs. "I downloaded porn. I find I quite enjoy having genitalia."

Remy might have laughed, but his breath was stolen as Pasha surged forward and licked his cool tongue from Remy's wet hole to his cock.

Remy grunted, his hips thrusting forward involuntarily as Pasha sucked his cock into his mouth. "Yeah… like that…" Remy encouraged, slipping a hand into the tin can's perfectly coiffed hair. He gripped tight, grinding his hips up and forcing Pasha's face down.

When Pasha hummed around Remy's cock, Remy shuddered and groaned.

The strange coolness of the android was more of a turn on than he'd have imagined. Remy was already so damn close to coming that he had to push Pasha back.

"Stop, stop…" Remy pushed until his mouth was off of him, and he looked up, Remy's juices glistening on his face. "Fuck me," He growled down at Pasha.

Pasha smirked and moved up, crawling over Remy until he was close enough for Remy to grab hold of the tin can's jaw, pulling him harshly forward into an aggressive kiss.

It grew harder, more passionate, as Remy grabbed at Pasha, pulling him further up until finally he was between his legs.

They were gasping into each other's mouths when Remy reached between them and took hold of Pasha's cock. It was as cool to the touch as the rest of him, and like the rest of him, he began to warm the longer Remy held it.

He pressed Pasha's cock against him and then pulled back a little to watch Pasha's face as he pushed inside.

And fuck, Pasha was beautiful. His face went slack with pleasure as he slid in.

"That's it, baby," Remy encouraged, pulling Pasha into another kiss. It took a moment for Pasha to reciprocate, lost in his own pleasure. Something that Remy hadn't realised would feel so fucking gratifying.

Pasha shifted, bracing himself a little more as he began to thrust gently, feeling his way through this new experience. And that was gratifying, too, not just being someone's first but being an android's first human. Something that would have sickened Remy not so long ago, now it was captivating.

Every sound from Pasha's mouth, every crease in his expression. It was so utterly beautiful watching his lover lose his virginity.

"Mmm, fuck. Need you…" Remy growled as he wrapped his legs around Pasha, urging him deeper, harder. And Pasha allowed himself to be guided, a slick wet sound filling the room as Pasha fucked into him.

With a grunt, Pasha buried his face in the crook of Remy's neck and began to nuzzle and kiss him there.

Not somewhere that Remy had been especially sensitive before, now it made him shiver at the intensity.

"This feels good," Pasha panted against his neck, at which Remy had to chuckle.

"Of course it does," Remy pumped his hips, meeting each thrust with a grunt, "It fucking does."

"Not just the sex, this…" Pasha near whispered as he pressed his cool lips to the pulse point on Remy's throat. His slightly dry tongue slipped out and licked over the artery with a whimper. "I can feel how alive you are. So warm and wet, it's like I can feel the blood flowing around your body."

Remy chuckled, Pasha's face contorting a little at how he constricted around him as a result. "You know, it's saying shit like that that makes people scared of tin cans like you."

Pasha slowed, pulled back, and looked down at his face, studying him for a moment. "Do I scare you, Remy?"

Remy reached up and caressed the android's face, the flesh that same cool warmth, a hint at the machinery within. "No, baby. I'm not scared of you."

Pasha leaned in and kissed him, resuming his motion so they rocked together. And fuck, the android felt good inside him. Not just the sensation of the inhuman flesh – which, who the fuck knew that would be such a turn on? But also the way Pasha explored him, adjusting here and there, changing rhythm. Trying to find an angle that pleased them both as he discovered what sex was like in practice.

The optimum position found, Remy cried out and dug his fingers into Pasha's back.

"There. There! I'm gonna come," Remy arched into the quickening thrusts.

Pasha was pounding into him; his eyes glazed slightly as he committed these moments to his memory files.

"That's it, baby," Remy encouraged as Pasha rested their foreheads together, fucking hard and fast yet still with so much tenderness and awe.

Remy couldn't wait for him to fucking come. He wanted to feel the release inside him and wondered what it would be like to have the green fluid slide back out afterwards. Just the thought of it, coupled with the friction of Pasha against his cock and inside him, had him on the brink.

"I want to feel what it's like when you come," Pasha gasped as he slipped a hand between them.

When he started to stroke Remy's dick expertly, Remy almost arched off the bed, his eyes rolling with pleasure and his entire body tensing.

Pasha grunted as he continued to fuck, continued to jerk off Remy and then—

"Fuck!" Remy cried out as Pasha's mouth returned to his neck, sucking a deep kiss over his carotid as though trying to connect with his life force. It was all so fucking good that Remy came, all the more turned on as wave after wave of orgasm hit, and he could feel himself clenching around the cock inside him.

In the end, he had to bat Pasha's hand away from his dick, which just encouraged the android to thrust all the more enthusiastically. He pumped his hips, fucking Remy's constricting, rippling inner muscles until, finally, he let out a surprised gasp.

Pasha's eyes were wide, his face frozen in pleasure as he experienced his first orgasm with another person.

Remy groaned as he felt Pasha spill. He'd never felt that before, not until it started leaking back out. But the coolness of the green liquid that seemed to be the android's life force was such a contrast in temperature that he felt every spurt of it. It was much colder than Pasha to the touch, and despite warming just as quickly as the android's flesh had, it made Remy gasp.

"Fuck that feels good," Remy groaned as he writhed against Pasha, his breath hitching every time it sparked a little more pleasure as his cock rubbed against Pasha.

"I didn't know it would feel like this…" Pasha replied in a gentle and awed tone.

"Like what?" Remy asked, wrapping his arms around Pasha as he collapsed on top of him.
"So… human."

Note: The primary focus of this story is Remy, however I am aware that this left little room to explore Pasha's non-binary identity, and potentially that of all androids. This was purely to keep the story contained within a word limit and is not meant to be dismissive of Pasha's identity. Had I spun this into a longer story or a novella then Pasha would have learned that he could present differently if he wanted, or change his pronouns. And maybe Pasha would, or maybe he'd find some other android way to ensure he is comfortable as who he is.

Creature Features

&

Furries

Intense Negotiations

For Kal, having carnal relations with werewolves is a religious experience.

Content Notes: Trans male vampire/cis male werewolf.
Vampires vs Werewolves! Mild power play, religious babbling, werewolf in human form, but even so: knotting. Implied full shift sex. Blood, biting.
Anatomical References: PIV penetration. Packer mentioned. Vague terms: hardness, lips, tight, and entrance used for trans male genitalia.

Kal walked into the bar and took a moment to scent the air, making sure it was worth his while staying.

This was the kind of place where people came for only one thing. And it was that one thing that he wanted. Sex.

But his desires were particular, not to mention taboo, and very much the draw of this particular establishment. It wouldn't do for Kal James, one of the leading clerics of *The United States Coven,* to be found in a place specifically intended to facilitate carnal relations between vampires and lycans.

Kal had been doing this secretly for years, and

that was only counting in human years. Way back before he started to work for the Coven and long before he began to progress towards leadership.

Back then, over a hundred years ago, before he'd even transitioned, it had been a lot harder. Until recent decades places like this had been illegal. Hooking up with a lycan had often required knowing the right people and the right parties. Though back then, it had less of a risk for him personally. He hadn't been anyone, another nameless and unknown face. One that eventually changed to the face he had now as he lived through decades of medical advancement.

Even so, Kal hadn't been *anyone* until he'd been deemed old enough to be initiated into the Coven, the selected few who governed the vampires in North America and by envoys across the globe.

As the years went on, it became easier to find places like this, but more dangerous for him. It had been prudent for Kal to become friendly with the owner of this bar and make deals to secure his anonymity. Luckily he was good at trading favours; he had enough sway in the vampiric commerce community to pull many strings when needed.

And now he stood trying to sense those around him for lycans. There was no point in him staying at this bar if there were none present, though he was prepared to wait a little while tonight. Longer than he usually might. Kal was particularly wound up and needed the release only being with a lycan could give him.

Tomorrow began the preliminary talks ahead of a peace summit between the US Coven and the *East*

European Lycan Enclave. And, given his position, he was to lead these initial discussions and pave the way for further negotiations. But the thought of spending that much time with werewolves already made his pants uncomfortably tight. A downside of his proclivities that made him thankful he would never usually encounter lycans in his daily life.

He definitely needed to fuck the feeling out of his system. They'd surely scent his arousal, and no one needed that while trying to bring peace between their people.

This evening, there were two lycans amongst the very few patrons. Kal could see one was already occupied in a booth at the back of the room, grinding a young female vampire against his clothed crotch. Kal ached at the sight and turned away, following the other scent to the bar.

Alone, there sat a sleek-looking beast. Kal would categorise all werewolves as beasts, but the word didn't quite fit in this case. The man was of a height with himself as far as he could tell from his perch on the stool. His dark hair was neatly styled, and his clothes – a button-up and fitted suit – were all black. From the side, Kal could make out sharp, almost angular features. He wasn't Kal's usual type at all, he had to admit.

Kal liked the big, thick-set alpha wolves who would hold him down and assert their dominance – at his command.

But there was something rather enticing about this man's scent and his vibe. He seemed calm and controlled, something Kal prided himself in being. It was why he had risen so high in the Coven and wasn't something he'd associate with most werewolves.

When the lycan moved slightly, his nose twitching, Kal knew he had also been scented and that his arousal was already apparent to all patrons in the room.

Kal began to approach the bar, and when the lycan turned to look at him, Kal could see the deep scar across his cheek. A battle scar of some sort, and Kal wondered if it had been dealt to him by a fellow lycan during infighting or a vampire during their ongoing wars. Either way, it made Kal shiver, saliva pooling in his mouth as he saw, as clear as day, an image of the blood gushing from the lycan's face before it was hastily stitched.

The lycan's gaze was dark. Not entirely hostile, but something near it. It seemed as though he wasn't sure if he wanted to appear approachable or not. Kal was willing to find out, taking the stool beside him along the empty bar and signalling for the bartender.

"You're wasting your time," the wolf rumbled at him, voice rich and deep with an accent that Kal would need more time to place.

"Excuse me?" Kal replied, his attention still on the bartender, who was now making his way over. The lycan remained quiet as Kal was served, not speaking again until Kal had taken a gulp of his o-negative-infused whiskey.

"I didn't know what sort of establishment this was when I first came in. I merely wished to have a drink." The lycan's words were cool and dripping in disdain.

Though Kal didn't miss the past tense there.

"Wished? Have your thoughts changed?" He latched onto the possibility and sipped his drink again, swirling the glass as he waited for an answer.

"A few minutes ago, I would have said no." The tone was almost put out, a resentment that he was rethinking his position, "Your scent is pleasing."

Kal's lips tweaked into a smile. "I enjoy yours too. You have no objections to being with men?" Kal ventured, having met some who did in the past. Lycans were often shorter in the tooth than vampires, and it was easy to forget how close they were to humans and their strange obsessions with binary attractions. Vampires had few hangups regarding gender or sexuality; having carnal relations with lycans was one of the few remaining taboos.

"No more than I do vampires," the lycan answered.

That drew a laugh from Kal, loosening his chest and making his skin hum. He is definitely not his usual type, but certainly an enticing character. The air practically crackled between them, and he'd never had that sort of immediate attraction with anyone before – lycan, vampire, or human.

"I have never been to a place such as this. What do people do if they find each other... acceptable?"

Kal swallowed, scenting that the lycan was becoming *very* interested in the idea. It was all he could do not to run a hand up the wolf's leg.

"Follow me," Kal replied, his voice husky with want. He hopped down from the bar stool and collected his drink before sauntering towards the back rooms, knowing with certainty that the lycan was following him.

Kal held the door for his new friend as they went into the back. It was a quick thing to show his membership card to the doorman and be allowed through to the long corridor of private, soundproofed rooms. Kal led the way down, finally opening the door of the first one that read as unoccupied.

Once inside, Kal held the door and watched the lycan hesitate before following inside with his drink. Kal slowly closed the door and slid the lock across in such an obvious way as to give the lycan time to object. When he didn't, Kal turned to look at his evening companion.

He had his back to Kal and was taking in the room, setting his drink on a sideboard. It was all luxurious fabrics and expensive aesthetics: a low coffee table and plush sofa, candles dotted on sideboards. The very back of the room was curtained but opened just enough to reveal the grand and sumptuous bed beyond.

Kal moved slowly around the lycan, taking the chance to look him over—the sleek lines of his jacket, the promise of an athletic form beneath.

He resisted the urge to run a hand over the expensive fabric of the suit. With any other, he might, but this lycan had been hesitant. He hadn't come here looking for this, and Kal didn't want him to change his mind. However, the growing scent of the lycan's arousal was clear and sharp. As was his own, drawing him forward.

"You want to fuck," the lycan said, cold and detached.

Kal stopped, grinning at the brazen comment—clearly a statement, not a question.

Kal turned to face the lycan completely, stepping into his space and leaning in to say, "Did you have other ideas?" His question was a low rumble.

The lycan huffed a laugh, and his brow was raised when Kal moved to look at him.

"I've never been with a vampire before," the lycan's grin was lopsided and somewhat condescending. There seemed an implication there that a vampire would be somehow lesser than someone with his own *superior* physiology.

Kal shook his head dismissively and walked away. Stalking back and forth in the space in front of the wolf, like he did when he made his impassioned sermons to the Coven. He knew the power he had; he knew how enigmatic he was. He didn't need to look at the lycan to know he felt it too.

"Some think," Kal began to sermonise, "that the vampire body is lesser than a werewolf, that it is only a rung above that of the human, given its similarity to that form. But scripture tells us," He looked to the lycan now, delivering the words to him directly, "that the first vampire was born of a demon and a human. That werewolves were spawned in the same way. And so, we are one. One flesh. Humans, vampires and lycans. Destined to find peace and—"

"Is that why you like to fuck with werewolves?" The lycan chuckled coldly, though Kal didn't miss the way the lycan's eyes roamed over his body, the way he ran his tongue out over a sharp tooth before continuing, "fuck your way to peace? An interesting strategy."

Kal joined with a peal of light laughter, a little self-deprecating as he shook his head.

"It isn't part of the scripture subscribed to by my kind or yours," Kal continued, "and no, I don't think coupling with werewolves brings us any closer to peace. But it does, personally, bring me closer to God."

Kal let out a shuddering breath and sucked his lower lip into his mouth as they stared each other down. The lycan was panting a little now too, and Kal knew – if he looked – he would see a hard outline in the black trousers.

"Every time I am one flesh with a wolf, I ascend a little further." Kal continued, breathless.

The wolf huffed, his grin sardonic, "Sounds like lycans are just better at fucking than vampires."

"That might also be true," Kal agreed with a growl and a smile. His movement was preternaturally quick, sliding his hand behind the lycan's nape and stepping up to him in one fluid motion, pressing their mouths together into a hungry kiss.

And it *was* hungry.

He could feel the lycan holding back and wondered if he could control his instincts, given that he seemed suddenly on the verge of shifting. Kal could sense it and practically feel its vibration against his senses.

It was everything he loved about being with a

lycan and more. Everything about *this* was so much more. All that harnessed power so close to exploding out into an animal form.

They drew back for breath.

"You're so cold," the lycan was finally able to say.

"Yes," Kal agreed, his ego rejoicing in being the first vampire this lycan had experienced.

"It's good…" The words came out like gravel, deeper than before. "I want to have you," the wolf growled against his lips, barely moving back to do so.

"For someone not looking for a hookup, you now seem pretty eager." Kal chuckled out the words, breathing them against the lycan's mouth.

"You changed my mind," he replied, his hand sliding between them so that he gripped Kal's crotch and continued, "As I said, I like your scent."

Kal moaned into the touch and pressed forward until his semi-hard packer was entirely in the lycan's hand, just the material of his pants separating them.

"Vampires don't submit," Kal rasped the words in the prideful tone that wasn't always well received amongst his own kind.

"Is that right?" The lycan huffed the words in amusement; a slight chuckle implied he might challenge that, but then he continued. "I wasn't aware I had asked you to submit."

"Just pre-empting," Kal said, then drew a deep gasp followed by a moan as the lycan's mouth moved to his throat and nipped.

Kal's body reacted instantly, an anticipatory

shiver over his skin at the knowledge that it would take little, even in human form, for the werewolf to do quite some damage if he chose to sink in his teeth.

It would unlikely kill him unless the beast beheaded him completely, but it would be a painful and lengthy recovery. And the thought of having such a threat hanging over him was profoundly arousing.

"Don't make me leash you," Kal growled, even as his hand went up to the lycan's nape, sliding into his hair and holding him at his throat, showing his equal strength.

A deep rumbling laugh responded, and the lycan spoke against the flesh he had been worrying with lips and teeth, "You're welcome to try."

The lycan had begun palming Kal's crotch, and with those words ringing in his ears, Kal was losing any remaining patience.

He growled as he took hold of the lycan's lapels and threw him bodily at the bed. It wasn't far, but all the same, it was far enough that the lycan looked up at him with a grin from where he now lay on his back, clearly amused and perhaps impressed.

"You're old," the wolf noted, a comment on his strength. "It's hard for me to tell with vampires."

Kal shook his head, "Not as old as some. Just... very capable."

It was true, another reason why he'd risen so high in the Coven. He'd quickly been taken under the Coven Master's wing and advanced in ways many his age would never have. He had the strength and skill of a vampire twice his age. And usually, the wisdom that went with it, aside from this little hobby. But, so long as it remained secret, he could go far.

The lycan's grin widened, and Kal's eyes went to the twitching bulge in the beast's trousers.

He scented the air and savoured it. Lycans always smelt so primal and base. Closer to the demon ancestry that the vampires were always trying to commune with. It seemed illogical to Kal that very few of his kind, especially those in his position, partook in this activity with lycans. Perhaps more would if they realised it achieved a greater closeness to God and the ancestors than any spiritual meeting or prayer.

"I won't be gentle," Kal said, both cool and heated at the same time as he advanced towards the bed whilst unbuckling his belt.

"I don't want you to be," The lycan replied, that grin still there. Combined with the penetrating stare, it seemed a taunt. He seemed to be daring Kal to do his very best. Or his very worst, depending on how it was categorised.

"So, you've not been with a vampire before," Kal acknowledged as he let his trousers drop, pulling them off with his shoes and socks.

The lycan shook his head, "The opportunity has never presented itself, and until tonight I had not been eager for it to do so."

Kal couldn't help but take pride in that, grinning as he pulled off his underwear and packer.

"Unlike many other vampires, you might find me different than you expect. You seem resilient, however. I am sure you'll cope," Kal grinned as the lycan's eyes followed his every movement, a hungry look there as Kal spread himself with his fingers and rubbed the hardness that peaked between his lips.

Hunger didn't leave those eyes, a sign to continue.

"Tell me," Kal asked as he moved to the end of the bed and began to unbuckle the lycan's belt, "do you believe in the worship of our ancestors?"

"No," the wolf replied plainly, "I believe in calculated odds and superior strategies."

Kal quirked his brow but couldn't help chuckling at the analytical response when he'd simply been attempting dirty talk. He opened the lycan's fly and pulled his trousers down just enough. The lycan groaned at Kal's cold touch and sank back onto the bed, looking at the ceiling.

"Are you going to make a believer of me?" the lycan rasped the words.

"Perhaps. Perhaps I can help you find God, as I have others before you." Kal breathed the words against the lycan's heated flesh as he leaned in to kiss and nuzzle, letting his fangs drop enough to graze the lycan's thick length.

The lycan let out a responding growl, and Kal felt sharp fingers sink into his hair and pull him back, yanking him hard until he met the lycan's gaze.

There was a possessive anger there, the expression of someone used to owning everything and being in control.

"Tonight, you are mine. You won't talk about others," the lycan's words were deep and commanding; they even made Kal shudder a little as he grinned in response.

"I may not usually take orders, but if it would ensure our coupling, I'll oblige."

The lycan snarled as Kal's frigid mouth pressed against him again, their eyes still locked.

"I admit, I am close to submitting," the wolf huffed a laugh, though he still seemed entirely in control of himself. Kal was almost tempted to see if he could push this one into losing himself, losing his control and triggering a non-lunar transformation.

Kal let him slip from his mouth with an audible pop, growling, "Don't let me stop you. By all means, lose control."

Kal moved quickly, rising onto the bed and straddling the lycan, his whole body thrumming with need as he hovered over the saliva-slicked cock.

"I'm going to use you, and you will enjoy it," Kal stated, getting only a grunt in response as he leaned in and pressed their mouths together in a rough kiss, rutting against him.

The lycan moaned and dug his fingers into the flesh at Kal's hips, claws protruding slightly.

Kal let out a self-satisfied groan.

"I thought you weren't going to submit to me?" The lycan growled, almost dazed in his pleasure as Kal rubbed himself along the length of his cock. Kal rocked until it was hitched at his entrance and left his new friend in no doubt of what would happen next.

Kal laughed, "This is not submission. I will take

what I want. I am in control. If you wolves think this is submission, then you are coupling incorrectly. Neither of us need submit at all."

He didn't give the lycan a chance to respond as he pinned him to the bed. Kal couldn't help but imagine the taste of the wolf's blood, and his heart thudded a little faster. He'd love to drink from this beast. Just a little. Just enough to feel him inside him in every possible way.

It was never like this with another vampire, almost as though vampires and werewolves were destined to come together just as they had once sprung together from the same inhumanly monstrous ancestors.

The wolf let out a strangled cry as Kal sank onto him. He was tight, he knew from the sound the wolf made, but he didn't give him a chance to adjust before he started fucking himself hard and fast on the wolf's cock. He gripped the clothed shoulders beneath him, looking down and watching as it took the wolf a moment to recover.

But once he had, his claws tightened, and he grunted as he let Kal use him. He didn't move, didn't thrust up. He submitted entirely, just clutching tight to Kal as though to keep a grip on the situation. One that he was rapidly losing as his Kal sensed the effort it was taking for the lycan to keep control.

The lycan's eyes rolled to the back of his head, and he shuddered, so close he might as well be sprouting fur. Kal gave him mercy and eased up a bit, slowing and not sinking so low.

"You're so cold," the lycan choked out the

words.

"You're so warm," Kal countered with a smirk.

"It's good…" The words came out like gravel, deeper than before. A hint at the control the wolf was losing.

"It's okay if you shift," Kal spoke as he picked up the pace again, the words panted and slightly obscured by his fangs extending in response to the thought of the man beneath him becoming the beast he truly was, mouth becoming a snarling muzzle, body muscular and furry. He'd tame the wolf into a giant teddy bear.

"Just warn me," Kal asked with a slight laugh. "I don't want to overreact and tear your throat out."

Kal imagined his face covered in the wolf's blood, and his heart thud a little faster, his teeth aching and inner muscles clenching. A tightening that drew an inhuman growl from the wolf and the constricting of his claws. They dug deep into Kal's flesh and drew blood. The scent of it aroused them both all the more.

So close to losing it, the lycan tried to move enough to take some control, but Kal slammed him back down to the bed, bunching his previously perfect dress shirt.

Kal braced his arm across the lycan's chest, ready to move it up to his throat as he fucked down on him hard and fast.

"I want you to think of our ancestors whilst you come inside me," Kal growled, noticing how the wolf's eyes flicked to his fangs.

He only received a grunt, one that spoke of a barely contained beast, as he pushed back, now fucking up into Kal.

"Oh fuck, that's it. Right there," Kal groaned as he took the lycan deep, pulled off again and then slammed back down. He didn't pull back again but took a breath before sinking to the absolute root of the lycan's cock. To the suggestion of a knot.

Everything was silent for a moment, and then the wolf let out a howl that Kal could feel from the chest under him. The wolf's whole body constricted as though he would curl in upon himself had Kal not been in the way.

His eyes were closed, but when he reopened them, they were yellow. Kal stopped the howl with a kiss, swallowing the noise within himself. Something primal and brought forth by his actions. It was a howl for him.

Kal felt it then, the push of that throbbing thickness and then the spill of come inside him that was so hot it was almost unbearable. It was never like this with another vampire; their seed was always so cold. Now the warmth that had radiated from having the lycan's cock inside him pulsed like molten liquid filling him.

The sensation was all Kal needed. He pulled back from the kiss, their mouths only millimetres apart.

"Oh yes, yes, all of it…" Kal commanded as he moved his hips, riding the friction it created. He felt the wolf's sharp breath as he came and tightened all the more, draining every last drop of him as the barely-there knot locked them together.

Kal chuckled, pulling back enough to look at him. His teeth had extended, but his muzzle had not, his eyes were wolflike, and his body was even hotter than before, burning with the need to fully shift that the lycan was barely managing to control.

"Impressive," Kal panted, "and challenging. Perhaps we can meet again and see if I can drive you to shift completely?" He leaned in and whispered next to the lycan's ear, "I do love the feeling of having one of you shift whilst inside me."

At that, as Kal had so predictably believed might be the case, the lycan snarled and surged up, rolling them so that Kal was now laughing beneath him. With a tug that bordered on painful, the lycan's wet and spent cock was against Kal's thigh.

"Don't like the thought of that, do you? You wolves are always so territorial."

At the call out, at the jibe, the lycan backed off a little, clearly realising that he had reacted precisely as Kal had wanted. That Kal was still very much in control even as he lay under him.

"Shift for me," Kal commanded softly.

Unlike many others, this one hesitated momentarily, not out of concern for Kal, he was sure of that. But hesitation at truly being that submissive, of being commanded in such a way.

But he did so, nonetheless.

Kal let out a satisfied hum as the air around them practically vibrated, and the lycan over him shifted. Bones crunched, and muscles expanded, ripping the lycan's remaining clothes. His muzzle extended, and his eyes were almost black, rimmed with that startling yellow, so much like the demons they had all once been.

When the shift was complete, and fur pressed

against him, Kal grinned.

"Good boy," he smirked. "Very good boy."

Kal rolled his shoulders, feeling the pleasant ache there.

He was so glad that he had indulged in his urges the night before. He could already scent the lycans arriving at the conference centre hired to host the talks. Without his previous romp and release, this would be hellish.

Kal closed his eyes and tried to block out the overwhelming scent. If he had not gotten it out of his system, he might even be getting a little aroused by their presence. And he couldn't afford that, not during these potentially historic talks.

Negotiations, really. Peace was the only option unless they wanted to spend yet another decade killing each other along poorly defined borders.

He watched the other Coven members, clearly affected by the scent in a completely different way. They shuffled their papers and seemed on edge by the beasts that were stalking towards the conference room.

"It'll be fine," Kal told them reassuringly. "Perhaps one soul at a time, we transform our broken world into a place that is whole again."

A few returned his smile, seeming a little comforted. They had a clear vision. They would attempt to connect with the lycans on common ground – their shared ancestry. They might not turn any of them to the scriptures from which the lycans had strayed so far, but they might find enough between them to broker a truce.

"Here they come."

Kal felt the energy around him rise.

The double doors were opened by venue staff, admitting the three representatives the Enclave had sent.

Nondescript for the most part. But for the third one.

As he walked through the door, Kal felt his blood run colder than usual. He had a deep sense of discomfort that he had rarely felt before. Only at times when he'd realised he might be out of his depth. Those infrequent times when he realised that he'd need more than charisma, bravado, and a good knowledge of the scriptures.

The lycan from the night before looked very different to how Kal had left him, sprawled on the bed exhausted, Kal's teeth marks on his thigh and blood smeared across his leg. Now he was before Kal, neatly dressed, all in black once more. And his scent was…

Kal cleared his throat as the lycans approached, reaching the other side of the large oval table. The lycan wasn't aroused, but there was *something* in his scent. A pleasure and amusement at seeing Kal again. Like he was smirking without his expression changing in the least.

Their place cards had already been set out, their names and titles. And there the lycan stood behind his: *Nikolai Hennigar – Commissioner*.

Kal turned his laughter inward before it could bubble up through him.

Commissioner, the title of the lycan overseeing the economic interests of the whole East European Enclave, and Kal had…

Kal smiled, feeling an immense sense of power in these negotiations that he might not have had if the night before hadn't happened.

"Pleased to meet you all," Kal said, holding his arms out in welcome and looking at the three before settling on Nikolai Hennigar.

The lycan smiled at him, an unexpected warmth there, a dark charm of his own.

"We're very much looking forward to these negotiations," Kal told them, letting a smile play across his lips.

"As are we," Hennigar growled back, the energy crackling between them with the promise of so many things to come.

Bloodthrall

Ben loves waking up next to his human girlfriend.

Content Notes: Trans male vampire/cis woman.
Vampires, biting, blood, blood drinking, issues
around consent and non-consensual siring, slight
transphobia. Mention of dysphoria.
Anatomical References: References to t-cock size
(substantial growth), PIV penetration, nipple play,
nipple sucking. Cock used for trans male genitalia.

Ben woke with a groan and stretched, feeling each
slight movement made by Felicia curled up to his
side. It was warm and comfortable, and Ben really
didn't want to leave the peace of it. So, he groaned
again. What was the point of having someone in
bloodthrall if he couldn't enjoy it? Or at least what
passed as bloodthrall these days in a much more
consensual day and age. A person willing to let you
drink from them, a friend or lover, or sometimes it
was simply a transactional relationship. What he'd
found with Felicia was something more than
friendship and certainly lovers; maybe one day, it
would be more.

A romantic at heart, he hoped that would be the
case. He was very fond of her and could easily

imagine himself in love with her. As much as a vampire could understand such emotions, their internal drives and desires were so different once turned.

Added to that was the fact that, in their months together, she had never asked him to turn her. She'd never even hinted at it. It was always so difficult when one's thrall was only there to find someone to turn them. It was off-putting to know that was their only interest in you, so there was no denying that Felicia was perfect for a vampire. Perfect for Ben.

But as they say, no rest for the wicked, and even vampires had to work for a living.

"I shouldn't stay over when you have to work," Felicia noted sleepily as she roused.

"I like you being here," Ben countered, burying his face in Felicia's abundance of thick hair. "I like waking with your scent on me, your warmth surrounding me." This was the closest he'd ever come to saying how much he cared for her, but he was sure she understood.

"You could just get a hot water bottle," she teased, but he shook his head. "Have more then," she offered, opening her arms to him so he could luxuriate for a few minutes more, "before you shower it off and go to work."

"All the more reason to have you again tonight," he growled, and at Felicia's knowing smile, Ben corrected, "Have you *stay* over, I mean."

Felicia chuckled, and Ben placed his mouth on her shoulder, gently scraping his teeth over prickling flesh.

"Yeah, I know what you mean," She moved

fluidly to straddle Ben, leaning down so that her hair fell like a voluminous curtain around them. "I like that you like to smell like me." Felicia smiled and circled her hips, already feeling Ben throbbing against her.

"Ugh…" Ben groaned and pushed onto his elbows, forcing Felicia to move backwards. Felicia sat up but didn't stop her grinding motions. Ben looked over at the clock and then fell back to the bed with another groan. "I need to leave in forty minutes. I can't…"

"You could forgo the shower. That will save twenty minutes," Felicia teased, now grinding fully onto Ben's small but hard cock. She never failed to turn him on. Their relationship had been instantly sexual, and when she'd discovered he was trans, she'd simply taken him into her warm, wet mouth and made him come.

But for now, he really did need to get ready for work, even if his efforts to push her away were lacklustre.

"And smell of you all night? Very professional." Ben tried to dissuade her.

He worked in night-finance for an international investments company, a member of the core team keeping everything running overnight whilst the markets on the other side of the world were open. Vampires had revolutionised the industry for those that could afford to hire them. Ben was sure none of his coworkers would appreciate him stinking of human all night, especially as most of them had chosen to abstain from human relations.

Felicia grinned, "Okay, breakfast. You can grab

a drive-through on your way. Or, you know, some jelly doughnuts or something." She teased.

Ben rolled his eyes even as his hands fell to Felicia's hips and started to guide the motion, giving in as they both knew he would.

"You gonna make it worth my while staying in bed a little longer?"

"When don't I?" Felicia replied, breathless, as she fell forward again, sinking her mouth onto Ben's and kissing him deeply.

"A quick one," Ben replied.

Felicia's delicate hand snaked between them and pushed his boxers down, sliding her fingers over his cock. He was hard, and she was an expert with his anatomy. She held him there, using her other hand to pull aside her panties and push Ben inside her.

They both moaned.

His hormone-grown cock was substantial compared to some but too small to go very far. Even so, the sensation was glorious, and he knew Felicia loved it too.

Felicia nipped at his lips as she started to ride him enthusiastically, their hips crushed together to take him as deep as possible while getting everything else she needed from the friction.

Ben's hands smoothed up from her hips to her breasts and cupped them, running his thumbs over Felicia's hard nipples. He wasn't sure she could ever get enough of Felicia's body. He loved it in a way that he'd never been able to love his own back before he had transitioned, before he'd been made vampire. He couldn't even consider how life would have been for him if he had been made immortal before he'd had the chance to transition. It wasn't even worth thinking about.

He shuddered and fought down the sudden wave of dysphoria. He had never been meant to have a body like this, but Felicia's body was perfection.

He concentrated only on thoughts of her and the months they had been together.

They clicked on so many levels of compatibility, and the first had been intimacy. There was more to their relationship, but it was something they both came back to. Neither of them had been this comfortable with someone ever before. The way they teased and played. Rough or gentle, even mundane morning sex, it was always so good. *So damn good.*

She really was perfect for him. Almost too good to be true!

Ben put his arms up around Felicia's back, drawing her forward so that she curved against him. He released the kiss and moved his mouth to her nipples. First one, then the other in a long suck before settling on her left nipple. Licking and sucking at it, feeling Felicia's hand move to her other to pinch it as she groaned.

Ben was already close, thrusting up so that Felicia practically bounced on him, never quite high enough for him to slip out, but enough for the friction to drive them both towards climax. Felicia was close, too. He could tell from her moans, how she ground against him, and how he could feel her throb and clench.

Ben bit at the flesh of her breast and then sucked a hickey a couple of inches above her nipple.

"Y-you can…" Felicia told him. This was all the encouragement he needed to sink his teeth lightly into her flesh. Enough to draw blood and suck it into his salivating mouth.

He struggled to keep control. He knew Felicia would happily be ravaged and feasted upon, but he really did need to get to work!

"More…" Felicia groaned as Ben licked and sucked until his saliva began to close the wounds, leaving just puncture scars.

Felicia held his head to her breast, panting as she continued to ride him. "Again," She demanded.

Ben shuddered but did as she asked, completely enthralled by the scent of her blood. Drunk on it. Even more so than usual.

He shook his head, trying to regain his senses, a sense of unease creeping over him.

"Please, Ben…" Felicia moaned, sliding down, repositioning herself so that her clit now rubbed against his cock, the sensation making them both shudder. "More…"

In a lustful haze, he bit again, harder than he meant to. Felicia cried out in pain, and blood flowed thick. He lapped and lapped, drinking it hungrily as his saliva stemmed the flow, and the wound began to close and scar.

Everything was strange and shadowy; the room seemed darker and the air oppressive as he tried to check that Felicia was okay, that he hadn't hurt her too much. But as he tried to speak, blood still thick on his tongue and coating his lips, nothing came out.

"It's okay," Felicia cooed as she stroked his hair

and continued to move her hips.

He could feel his hardness flagging, all his muscles draining of strength, as she began to slow.

"Wha—" he tried to ask, but it was just a mumble, his mouth slack. He felt heavy, sinking into the bed whilst barely being able to feel the bedding around him—like he was floating. He could no longer feel Felicia; he couldn't feel anything.

She must have moved because she was gone as he tried to focus. His eyes drooped shut, and when he managed to open them again, she was back. This time she was sitting next to him, something in her mouth.

His arm.

He tried to protest. He tried to cry out and move away but was utterly immobile.

"Don't worry," she told him softly, "it will wear off in a few hours. I didn't realise it would take so long to work! Too risky to give you a big dose. I can't believe it has taken all this time to kick in, finally." There was something cold in her tone, chilling and detached, so unlike Felicia. "You seemed to waver for a moment when you fed last night. I thought it would be then."

She was petting him as she spoke, holding his arm delicately, even pressing kisses to it. Blood smeared across her mouth from where she drank from the cut he couldn't feel.

No.

He wanted to stop her, but his eyes began to close again.

He could hear her gentle words.

"Don't worry about anything. Don't worry about work. I have other plans for you."

When Ben woke up, it was daytime – the blackout blinds had been drawn, and the usual glow around their edges made clear it was a sunny day.

He was still in the bed, naked and covered in his and Felicia's blood.

He was hesitant before trying to move to find out if he was alone. But when he gripped the blankets beneath him in his hand, it was clear sensation had returned. His body still felt heavy, his head felt light, and he knew that was because of the amount of blood Felicia would have had to take in order to turn.

He shuddered as he remembered his own involuntary siring.

He'd been such a fool. He should have abstained like the others. He'd heard all the horror stories of humans that get too attached or only want to be with a vampire to get turned for some romantic notion. He was so sure that hadn't been the case with Felicia. Sweet, gentle Felicia.

He'd heard the stories about groups of humans who wanted to be turned for more nefarious reasons. Criminals who would then enslave their sires. He'd never believed that could be true. And there was no possible way he could have imagined Felicia to be one of them, but now he had to consider that he had never really known her at all.

The door to the bedroom opened, and an

unfamiliar shadow appeared in the doorway. It wasn't until she moved into the room that he realised it was Felicia – her hair no longer free-flowing curls but pulled back into a tight bun, making her look severe and hard. She wore tight-fitting vest and pants, such a change from her usual billowy skirts. And the thing was, this look suited her. This was the real her, not just the result of being made a vampire.

This had been her all along, and he'd never damn well seen it.

"Felicia?" His throat was tight, and the word came out as a croak. When he swallowed he felt a physical tightness too. One he couldn't make sense of until she came closer and picked something up from the side of the bed. With a sharp tug, he was on the floor, a chain attached to a thick leather collar at his throat in her hand.

She tugged on it again until he was essentially to heel, looking up at her.

"You were a lot of work! I thought you'd be easier. That I wouldn't even need to resort to spiking my blood."

"Why me?" The question bounced around Ben's brain until he said it out loud. Because he had clearly been chosen for whatever this was. Targeted. And that thought made his blood run colder than it naturally did.

"I thought you'd be weak," Felicia chuckled and shook her head. "I thought you'd be easy to control." Her newly sharp teeth flashed at him. "Broken. Pathetic. But you weren't. I think at some point, perversely, I began to enjoy the challenge."

She tugged the chain again, and he didn't resist, feeling her strength, trying to gauge it as well as he could. It was ample, though nothing compared to his, and she'd have realised that if they'd grown even closer, close enough for him to show her exactly how much he was holding back to ensure her safety. Weak, broken, pathetic? That's what she had thought.

The smile didn't reach his lips but lodged in his chest, a warm feeling like having a heart again. Like remembering what it was to be a vampire and not this tame thing that society wanted them to be to fit in.

He had never abstained like so many others, and drugged or not, her human blood had given him a strength that abstainers would not have.

But being a vampire wasn't the thing that had made him strong. Being trans in a world that hated him for all those years before he had turned was where his strength had come from. That was something she would never understand.

He would allow her one day. One day for the drugs to be gone, and one day to get to know the real person she had been concealing all this time. Find the weaknesses she would inevitably no longer try to hide now that she was a vampire with all that new strength coursing through her.

One day. And then he would turn the tables, and she would live to regret the day they had met.

A HalFLaMb SacriFice

Joshua believes he is prepared for his fate.

Content Notes: Trans man/cis male monster.
Fantasy, human sacrifice, virgin sacrifice, arguably
non-consensual touching (initially), references to
cannibalism, oral sex and fingering.
Anatomical References: References to having
been assigned female at birth. Vague terms: wet,
taste and flavour used for trans male genitalia.

Joshua knew they would come for him sooner or
later. He was the last female of his bloodline, or he
had been born so. They had been saving him for a
bad year. And this year had been dire indeed. The
crops had failed completely. Without a sacrifice, the
village was doomed.

His dad tried to bar the door when they came for
him, but Joshua touched his arm gently. "It's ok,
Dad. We knew this would happen someday. I'm
ready."

And he was.

He would go to a dignified end like most of the
girls had. He wasn't going to try and fight it and
have hysterics over an unchangeable fate as Elaina
had six years ago. Her screams had made it so much

harder for the village. They did this to keep the village alive. It was selfish for anyone to put themselves above the whole village in that way.

His dad cried silently but nodded and followed along to say goodbye. Once they reached Sacrifice Hill, he embraced his father and wished him well.

"I'm doing this for all of you. Please stay safe." He squeezed his dad tight before releasing him, turning away and allowing the two priests to lead him up the hill. Near the top, he was stopped at the small hut where he was allowed to change from his clothes into the loose ceremonial robes worn by the sacrifice – it had been woven by the villagers with scenes of good crops and sunshine and given sacred blessings.

The priests gave him sorrowful and sympathetic looks as he climbed onto the altar and lay back on the cold stone so the ropes could be tied to his wrists and ankles. A tradition, really. Perhaps in the past, the sacrifices had struggled. He wasn't going anywhere. He'd accepted that this would be his fate long ago.

Joshua could see the torches burning at the bottom of the hill, but one by one, they left. He was sure the one that stayed the longest was his father. But eventually, they were all gone, and the sky was pitch black.

There was silence, not even the noise of nocturnal animals—only his own soft breathing in the darkness. Joshua was near nodding off when a sensation woke him. He sensed someone standing close to him and then the pull of air at his throat as he was scented. It sent a shiver through him, and he turned to see who or what was there.

There was something, but he could not see the coal-black flesh against the dark sky. Then burning red eyes fluttered open close to his face. Joshua gasped a breath and drew back as far as his bindings would allow.

"Hmm, they haven't sent me a male before..." The words were a deep rumble from a red mouth that split the burn-charred-looking skin. The creature straightened and placed his hand on Joshua's shoulder, dragging it down to his ankle as he walked the length of the altar.

"Please great beast... please, uh..." Joshua tried to remember the words, the dedication with which he was meant to offer himself up, but the hand tickling lightly at his ankle sent an intense pull through his nerves. "... take my flesh and bless the village with your bounty."

A dark chuckle rumbled through the air, and the hand snaked slowly up to his calf under the robe. Joshua's breath hitched. The soft and tender touch should have made it all the more terrifying.

"I try to tell them every year... dear boy, I have lived here in this realm longer than the village has had stone houses. Once, I had a name, wealth, and power before I grew into this form. But never have I had the ability to bring the rains or raise the crops. Nor would I want it. But as they keep giving me such tender and willing flesh for my table, who am I to refute your backward ideas." Another deep chuckle.

"You did something. Wronged the fae or a witch." Joshua considered aloud at the mention of this great beast once having a name. The fae trapped people by their names. "Your name traps you. Whoever has it can control the beast you have become."

The beast chuckled, "Astute as well as beautiful."

Joshua frowned. "You do not raise the crops, but you mean to eat me, even so."

"Even so. Yes." The beast replied.

The hand was at Joshua's knee now, and he squeezed his eyes shut and shuddered.

"You are quite tender. I believe I would like to taste you." The beast shifted then, but Joshua wasn't sure where it was in the dark until he felt a wet, warm mouth on the robe over his crotch. He uttered a small cry and jerked his hips, unsure whether he was trying to press forward or pull away. Long fingers pushed his hips down as the beast pressed his face into the folds of fabric, dislodging them until they fell away and he could taste flesh.

Joshua knew he should be scared. He may have accepted his fate, but in truth, when he had been tied to the altar, he had been terrified. He had been terrified right up until the beast spoke in a soft, charming voice.

Air left his lungs as the beast took Joshua's small cock into his mouth. He felt as if he would melt into the cold stone. "What sorcery is this then?" he panted, knowing he could not really feel this way. So warm, relaxed. Safe. The beast pulled back, and cold air hit Joshua's oversensitive cock, sending a jolt through him, that place between his legs growing wet.

"I told you, I have no magic. I merely am." The words were soft as the beast ran fingers lightly over Joshua's thigh. Joshua instinctively tried to spread his legs but was held tight by his bonds. The beast murmured an amused and approving hum. "I enjoy the way you taste. Perhaps I can have more?"

Joshua felt the hand at the inside of his thigh running slowly upwards, towards a place that, for the first time, now ached to be touched.

"Yes…" Joshua breathed the word, groaning as the beast's fingers found him wet, and slid slowly and deep within him. Joshua flinched against his bonds and winced as rope bit into his skin.

"Relax, darling boy." The words were as gentle and tender as the fingers that moved within him and caused a spark of pleasure through his entire body. Joshua had no breath left, his lungs burned as the fingers withdrew, and he heard more than saw the beast place them in his mouth. "You have a delightful flavour. It would be a shame to waste it on one good meal if I could taste it indefinitely instead."

The beast's fingers played over Joshua's thigh again, and then a long finger trailed over his hard cock.

"Aren't you going to eat me then?" Joshua asked, not entirely fearful of the answer.

"In a manner of speaking, perhaps." A light and amused tone there. "Every year, I am sent sacrifices to appease magic I do not possess. Nonetheless, I am not so rude as to refuse a gift, so I feast on them as is intended. You are unlike those others. You ignite something within me that has been long cold.

I find myself willing to strike a bargain with you…"

The beast's hands were gone from him then, and Joshua felt the loss keenly. They were tugging at the ropes a moment later, testing the bonds that held him.

"What is your name, boy?"

"Joshua… Joshua Halflamb." His breath caught every time a new rope was tested, and the beast was gone again. There was silence for several long minutes. Joshua tried to steady his breathing; the chill air playing across his exposed lower half made him ache for another gentle touch.

"Joshua…" The beast breathed out his name as though he were tasting it on his tongue. "Come with me to my home, and I will care for you in every way you require. One year from this day, you may choose to be consumed in place of the next sacrifice to be tied here as you should be tonight. Or you may choose to consume them alongside me."

Joshua's breath hitched. "You can't ask that, I…"

"I ask you to spend a year with me, nothing more. The choice at the end is yours to make, unless, of course, you believe you can change me in that time. Tame me?" There was a smile in those words, but they felt like an invitation even so, perhaps even a challenge.

"One year." Joshua agreed. "But I have my own condition."

"Name it." The beast seemed breathless, elated.

"If I stay, after the year, will you…" he hesitated. He shouldn't want this. He had never wanted this before with anyone in the village. But he had always known this would be his fate – he would belong to this beast either way. "Will you tell me your name?"

A soft chuckle then as he felt the first rope holding him come loose. "I don't think I'd be able to stop myself."

Carnivorous

Jason is finally going to meet the lion he's been talking with.

Content Notes: Trans male/Trans male.
Furries, fursuits, references to animalistic cock sheaths, vore, consensual cannibalism. Implied murder and non-consensual cannibalism.
Anatomical References: Packer, metoidioplasty (meta), blow job on a meta penis, penetration with a meta penis. Hard, wet, entrance, hole, t-cock and cock used for trans male genitalia.

Jason adjusted his fursuit and eyed himself in the mirror one last time. He would be easy to spot. Ferrets weren't common at these events, he found. Often lots of canine types, sometimes big cats. He hoped there wouldn't be too many lions. He wanted his to be easy to spot.

One last look before leaving the hotel room and going to the suite where the private furry gathering was held this month. A different city each time; he'd only made it to those closest to him until now. But with the promise of something special, he had made the trip from New York to Baton Rouge without hesitation. He didn't take much time off from his job on the force, but when the sergeant had casually asked if he had nice plans, Jason had just muttered enough about *trans stuff* for the man to nod and walk off. This wasn't something he ever really wanted his colleagues to know about. It was one thing being out and hopeful that HR would deal with any bullshit; it was another to reveal *this* part of himself.

For sure, plenty of cops had their secret kinks – being a furry probably wasn't even that risqué. And vore roleplay wasn't uncommon amongst furries, but there were limits. Or there had been until Jason had found someone without such compunction. The lion in question he only knew by the online name— King. His fursona profile picture was furry art of a lion with bloody jaws and a giant, hard cock.

They had talked online for a few weeks before vore came up and many weeks more before they discussed the reality of it. A taboo, really. Vore was play. It wasn't for real – a roleplay where they might act it out, nothing more. And yet... Jason's breath caught at the memory of having gently cut a small square of his flesh from the inside of his upper arm. It had healed much as scarification, and the thought of it made him hard and wet. He had sent it to the PO Box King had provided and received in return photos of the flesh on a tongue, another of it between sharp teeth. A note saying he was delicious and a request to taste more.

The *more* wouldn't happen today. No, this was to meet and arrange something more private if all went well. Jason wasn't sure how far they would go. He knew what he wanted – a taste in return, at the least. And those teeth on him, regardless of whether there was any devouring. The threat of them was enough to make him want to come.

Jason shook the thoughts from his head as he knocked on the door to the private suite.

He'd had these desires as long as he could remember—*consumption*. But never before had he found someone willing. It was the thing that had drawn him into the furry fandom—the possibility of sharing his vore fantasies and taking them further if he was honest.

The room was already full, perhaps thirty or so guests in total. A small gathering compared to conventions, but everyone was in fursuits – an expensive pursuit. The room stank of that particular kind of musky yet pleasant sweat that came with the outfits. The host he had met at a previous party, an otter called Slip. He showed him around and introduced him to a few others he hadn't met.

The suite had three bedrooms leading from the central lounge area, two of which had handwritten signs stuck to them saying, "If the door is closed, Yiffing in progress." Someone had scrawled "so come on in" and a smiley face under one of them.

The parties weren't all like this, but he knew Slip's reputation and wasn't surprised. People joked his name was short for Slippery, which Jason was unsure of, but he did know the guy came across like a used car salesman, though he had once been told that Slip was, in fact, some affluent entrepreneur. Those real-world identities didn't matter once the suits were on.

A few people were dancing slowly to some

music, and the balcony door was open, letting in the cooling breeze as the sun went down. There appeared to be a cuddle pile happening on the large sofa. Jason felt relaxed. He felt at home in a way that he didn't in any other aspect of his life. This community had always been welcoming of him, and his gender had never been an issue.

Jason had only gone in for yiffing a couple of times before when he'd been particularly lonely and needed to feel more than just warm fur against his own. He'd let himself be fucked hard by a wolf once, and by a horse who had insisted on wearing a cock sheath that made him more equine in that department. Jason wasn't much into that sort of thing, but he'd still come hard with the massive cock inside him as he grew wet to excess.

He bit his lip at the memory and looked around the room, vision a little impaired by his headpiece.

"I'm looking for a lion called King. Do you know him?" He asked Slip.

"Oh! King, yeah. He'll be here later. He always likes to wait for the party to get started. He's a bit pretentious but nice enough. Well liked." Slip sounded almost bitter about it, jealous.

Jason nodded and left it at that. He mingled, allowing some old acquaintances to pet him and draw him into a cuddle pile. The closeness was welcome but not what he wanted or needed. Even so, it gave him a clear view of the door, allowing him to see an hour later when a lion arrived.

Majestic, fucking beautiful. And easily the most expensive fursuit Jason had ever seen by a long mile. King moved effortlessly into the room, talking and shaking hands, easy and comfortable with the company. Jason felt a little of that jealousy that Slip did. Maybe at that ease of King's casual sociability or perhaps because he was not yet the recipient of it.

But then King saw him and made his way over.

"Charmer?" He asked, and Jason nodded, extricating himself from the cuddle pile and standing to face the lion. King chuckled. "As beautiful as I expected," the words were rich and deep, catching Jason off guard. He hadn't even considered how much more overwhelming it would finally be to meet in person.

Jason tried to join the chuckle but knew his nerves were evident.

"Shall we?" King asked, holding an arm and pointing to the less crowded balcony. Jason nodded and slipped his arm into the crook of the lion's.

They found a spot to lean against the railing and look over the city. "Thank you for the gift you sent me." King moved as he said it, warmth radiating from him even as the cool breeze blew around them.

Heat flushed Jason's skin, but he was glad the lion couldn't see it.

"Perhaps we can talk about limits? Desires?" King suggested as Jason continued to be rendered mute by the lion's presence.

Jason nodded.

"In private?" King asked. Jason nodded again. "I will find you later." The lion said, stroking a hand down the side of Jason's ferret face before he turned and walked off.

Jason gasped in the air, suddenly breathless, as he watched King start to socialise again. He rejoined the cuddle pile, anxious for the comfort of it as he watched the lion stalk the room and talk and laugh with other guests for the next two hours.

"Apologies, I haven't attended in a while, and it would have been rude not to reacquaint myself." King lowered himself into the sofa next to Jason, the pile shifting to allow it but resulting in them being pressed together.

"Th-that's ok." Jason managed; nothing but nerves left.

King crowded in towards him. "Somewhere private then?"

Jason swallowed and nodded. "My room... I have a room downstairs."

King seemed to hesitate for a moment. "I actually live nearby. If that isn't too forward? I assure you, you are perfectly safe with me. I can have Slip vouch for me."

Jason was instantly torn. Uncertain about going somewhere so private but filled with a desire to do just that. He was good at reading people, which made him a good cop, but he couldn't read a man in a costume. "My room first? Then maybe?"

"Of course," King replied and got to his feet, pulling Jason up and holding him close as he walked them from the suite, jealousy conspicuously rising behind them, conspicuous even through the suits.

Once in his room, Jason felt a little more confident. Being away from prying eyes. King closed the door behind him, and they faced each other.

"Your suit is magnificent. I knew it would be. I could taste it in your flesh." King's voice was a low growl and practically pulled a purr from Jason.

Jason closed the distance between them then and lifted his hands, tentative as he drew off the lion's head, waiting to be stopped, but he wasn't. He wanted to see the man's face and read him. He wanted to see those teeth. To feel them.

The man was stunning. The mouth was familiar from the pictures, but his eyes were deep and dark, his cheekbones sharp. Jason let out a breath and placed the lion's head on the bed before lifting off his own head, knowing his curls would be mussed from sweat. He was nervous as he revealed himself.

King watched him hungrily as he set his head down next to the lion's.

"Charming indeed."

"I want your teeth on me," Jason blurted, his heart racing as the words escaped.

King walked him back to the bed and pushed him onto it, covering Jason with his body as he rutted against him. Jason groaned as teeth nuzzled into his throat.

They ground against each other, neither wanting to halt and remove layers or do anything more as King made Jason's throat and neck painfully raw with his teeth. The suits added to the friction as both remained trapped inside their own.

Jason grew wetter and wetter until he was sure

his suit was getting damp but was too caught up in the moment, in this desperate need, to try to undress. Instead, he arched and moaned until the lion pulled back and allowed him to spread his legs, which he did readily.

Jason held back pleas as they rutted against each other, his soft packer creating as much friction as he needed, despite the layers of fur between them.

When King pressed against him and bit gently at the side of his neck, holding him in place as a lion might when mounting, Jason came with a cry. King grunted and held Jason down as he rutted against his pliant form, fucking against him until he, too, came.

They lay panting, King's weight pressing him down in a way that comforted Jason so entirely he had to resist pulling the lion's arms around him.

"Let's go to your place." Jason managed to say breathlessly.

Jason had grabbed his shoulder bag and packed some fresh clothes before they went down to the basement parking lot still in their fursuits, now soiled from their release. It made for an uncomfortable but thankfully short drive.

The apartment was neat and expensively furnished, which wasn't a massive surprise given the quality of King's fursuit. They had gone unseen through the parking lot beneath the building and were alone in the state-of-the-art kitchen.

Was this where King had cooked his flesh?

"Can I get you something to eat or drink?"

Jason shook his head, flushing at the idea of his flesh. He hesitated before asking, "Are you on the menu?"

King grinned. "It would only be fair. An eye for an eye... a tooth for a tooth." King pressed a now ungloved thumb into Jason's mouth, and he sucked and nipped at it with a moan. "But... perhaps first, if you permit me, I'd love to see the Charmer beneath the suit?"

Jason nodded and chased King's thumb as he removed it before being led into a lavish bedroom.

The lion's hands were gentle as they unzipped Jason's suit but didn't push it off, revealing the naked flesh beneath as it peeled down to his waist.

"Touch me," Jason muttered, his breath catching when King's hand dipped down the front of his suit and into his underwear, finding him wet beneath his soft packer.

"Oh," the word was followed by a grin, "how very interesting."

Fingers expertly stroked him, the tips sliding against his entrance as Jason shivered. Minutes of gentle caress made his knees weak until finally, King pulled him out of his suit entirely, drinking in the sight. Jason stepped out of the last of it, now just in his damp underwear.

"I want to fuck you. Is that ok?" King's voice was thick with lust. Jason nodded and moved forward, helping the lion out of his costume to find him naked beneath but for substantially filled underwear. "But first... a taste for you?" King slipped his hand into his underwear as he went to the bed, lowering himself down onto his back and offering a hand to Jason.

Jason took King's free hand and allowed himself to be pulled between the lion's legs and then manoeuvred down until he understood. He kissed the trail of golden hair running from King's navel, continuing down as King pushed his bulky underwear to his thighs.

Jason nuzzled and kissed, running his tongue down until—

He moved back onto his haunches, looking down at the sight beneath him, spread legs revealing a wet hole and thick, throbbing t-cock.

"Very interesting," Jason muttered, echoing King's words.

Without hesitation, Jason lowered his mouth to King's cock, running his tongue up it before sucking it into his mouth. He had never done this before, but guided by what he found pleasurable himself and the deep, throaty noises above him, he was sure he was doing well.

Even more so when King's hand went to his head, gripping his thick dark hair as he rut against Jason's face. He was a little larger than Jason; he'd had meta surgery where Jason had not. Released from the flesh beneath it, it stood erect in a way Jason's could not and whilst he was happy with his own body and not jealous, he was deeply curious.

"Can you fuck me? Without a toy?" Jason asked, breathless, as he pulled back to stroke King's cock between his fingers.

King answered with actions rather than words, letting out a guttural moan before taking hold of

Jason and rolling in the large bed.

Once King was on top, Jason spread his thighs for the lion, accepting the hungry kisses as he pressed their cocks together and rut once more. Ample wetness between them; Jason was already hard and aching when King sat back and grabbed a pillow. He moved it under Jason's hips before positioning himself.

Jason couldn't hold back the soft cry as he felt King's wet cock slide back and forth over his own and then down to his entrance.

They both held their breath as King pressed forward and sank into him, thick and long enough to spark all the sensitive flesh inside him.

"Oh fuck," Jason moaned, his head falling back. "That feels so good."

With a grunt, King moved, retreating a little so that he slid almost the whole way out and back in again. He repeated the action slowly, sliding out fully more than once before finally sinking into him and pressing their bodies tight together.

Jason hiked up his legs, his own hard cock rubbing against King as he pumped into him repeatedly, their mouths so close together that they were panting the same breath. It was the most sensual, intimate sexual experience Jason could ever recall experiencing, and he wanted more.

"Will you come?" King asked, through a laboured breath.

Jason nodded mutely, his mouth hanging open as every thrust sent flashes of pleasure through him.

Their hips pressed together, their bodies moving as one; the bed creaked beneath them until they were just a messy tangle of limbs, and the rhythm faltered.

Jason came with a cry as he felt King throbbing inside him, felt the press of teeth at the side of his neck and heard the deep animalistic growl next to his ear. They fucked through their shared orgasm, riding the waves of it until they collapsed onto each other, both spent.

Jason whimpered at the loss when King finally pulled off him.

He didn't want to lose this connection, this visceral way they had explored each other, knowing only of one other experience that paralleled this intimacy.

"A taste, please. Let me devour you?"

King chuckled. "Such a sweet ferret, a deceptively cute carnivore." He took Jason's lips in a hard kiss, pleasantly bruising.

"You can taste me if you wish, but I have a proposal," King growled the words in a way that vibrated through Jason.

"Yes," he breathed, ready to be convinced of anything King might ask.

King stood and drew him from the bed, leading him naked back to the kitchen. "When we started talking, I knew immediately that I had found someone with a shared desire, common predilections. I hope I have not been mistaken." There was a faint note of something like a threat in those words, yet Jason wasn't scared.

King led him to a door off the kitchen, storage, he presumed. But when it opened, within, there was a wall of wine bottles and, concealed behind that, a smaller second kitchen. The stark lights lit everything, including the sterile butcher's table. Jason's heart was thudding in his chest, he should be scared, but instead, he was excited.

In truth, he had given King a taste to have something in return; he desired to consume as well as be consumed. He was willing to allow some give and take. With the butchery equipment set up before them, he was unsure who would eat who, and he knew that should worry him. But he realised with no fear that this lion had his devotion before they had even met in person.

King let go of his hand and moved to a fridge. He pulled something out that Jason couldn't see until he turned back and placed it on the chopping board.

A neatly cut human leg and foot cut beneath the knee.

Jason's breath caught, and his heart raced. They looked at each other for a moment, assessing, seeing each other clearly in the stark light.

"Perhaps this is something we can enjoy together? I have a fantastic recipe I've been meaning to try."

Note: This is a work of fiction and not intended to imply that furries are murderers and/or cannibals. Cops, on the other hand…

The Inevitable Tentacles

Semiaquatic

Will a bar hook-up with a non-binary otter help Byron with his own identity issues?

Content Notes: Non-binary otter/cis male bull
Anthropomorphised animals, masc non-binary character, loneliness, bar hook-ups, body consciousness, body issues, identity issues, therapeutic sex toys, tentacle sheath toy, anal fingering, anal sex, profanities, doggy-style, multiple orgasms.
Anatomical References: References only to anal sex.

By The Sea Bar was exactly that: a cruising bar just up from the stretch of beach where the ocean met the mouth of the river. The location made it especially popular with otters, bears, muskrats, and the occasional seal. This far out from the countryside, it wasn't exactly the sort of place that saw many patrons that weren't semiaquatic, especially bovines.

Byron nervously tapped a hoof on the floor as he nursed his beer at the bar. The few times he had seen other pastural types happen by, they were pretty successful in their hookup attempts. But then, they had actually hit on patrons and made it happen. Byron was still working his way up to that.

Maybe tonight he would get up the nerve to try and hit on someone?

The beautiful otter at the end of the bar, for example.

Byron had seen the otter there before. He always had a lonely vibe about him, even though he was constantly hooking up—usually with bears. He would disappear into the back room and come back out with a satisfied expression that didn't entirely cover the loneliness there. Byron could relate—in as far as the loneliness, not so much the hooking up. He was sure he wouldn't feel lonely if he went into the back room with the otter.

But Byron wasn't his type, he was sure.

Byron wasn't a grizzly; he wasn't anything that mattered. A bull with so many issues that they might as well be etched into his horns for everyone to read. Even other bulls didn't want him.

The otter was beautiful. His clothes, which sat perfectly on every inch of his lithe body, were androgynous. And something about how he carried himself exuded both a masculine and feminine energy. He was by far the most beautiful creature in the bar.

Byron sighed, torturing himself with thoughts of *what if.*

The thoughts were enough to have *it* stirring, and Byron felt heat rise on his cheeks, creeping almost all the way up to his horns.

No one would ever want him, no matter how lonely they might seem. And the chances were, the otter's loneliness was simply all in Byron's mind. A sweet fantasy to try and trick him into believing he might have something in common with such a beauty.

Byron drank down the rest of his beer and ordered another. The bittersweet torture was better than going home sober and alone.

The corridor back from the bathroom was narrow and dimly lit. Byron was already tipsy, making it hard to avoid bumping into the people lingering there on their way to or from one of the back rooms.

There were several people pressed against the wall, kissing and touching. Byron received annoyed glances and harsh words as he passed, disturbing other people's fun as he tried to shuffle through like the clumsy oaf he knew himself to be.

Byron wasn't sure why he kept doing this to himself.

He wasn't really what anyone was looking for. And perhaps there was a comfort in that, allowing him to convince himself that it wasn't personal that no one was interested in a bull, even though he knew the lie in it.

It was an easier rejection than the ones he'd had all his life.

Byron had known early on that he was different from all the other teenage bulls, even before his first sexual encounter. And that had been disastrous, a precursor to the rest of his infrequent sexual history over the years.

Byron sighed and tried to squeeze his way down the corridor.

"Watch it," came a huffed but somewhat amused voice as he collided lightly with someone—or rather, someone collided with him.

It was the otter, and this close, Byron could breathe in his scent. It was rich and earthy with a hint of sea salt. It made Byron shudder with want, his imagination supplying the image of the otter's fur wet with water as he waded from the sea and onto the beach.

The otter moved quickly around Byron, continuing to the bathrooms, or maybe the back room, without a backward glance.

Byron sighed again, torn for a moment. He could go home and cry, or sink into another pint or two, hoping to feel numb about his situation.

He chose the beer and sat there nursing it for long minutes before someone appeared beside him.

"Hey, sorry. I'm kind of a shit when… Oh, it doesn't matter. Just wanted to say sorry for knocking into you."

It took Byron a moment to realise the otter was talking to him. He looked up, stunned, as the otter slid into the seat next to him at the bar.

"Don't you just find all this shit depressing?" He chuckled. "I think I've had every bear in this place, and almost everyone else too, but…" He shrugged. "Is it possible to get bored of backroom sex?"

Byron remained silent, unsure whether it was a rhetorical question. Eventually, the otter continued.

"Don't see many bulls here. Not exactly the semiaquatic clientele that usually frequents this place." It wasn't a question, but there was something leading in those words, and Byron knew he should answer.

He swallowed.

"I, um, I live near here," Byron explained. Not a lie, but not the reason he came to this place. Somewhere more comfortable than the sort of places a bull might usually go.

The otter raised a brow but didn't question further, signalling to the beaver behind the bar instead and having a drink set in front of him.

They lapsed into silence, the otter swirling the last of his drink before downing it and sighing.

"I think I'm just getting jaded with all this shit." He let out a dark chuckle.

Byron had no idea how to answer. His social skills weren't exactly fantastic when he approached someone, but to have the object of many of his fantasies now sitting next to him and trying to make conversation, Byron was at a complete loss for words.

He frowned and licked his lips, trying to find something to say.

"You are very morose." Byron finally managed.

The otter cocked a brow at him and then let out a bark of laughter. He laughed until he shook and slapped Byron on the back, releasing another waft of that scent as he did.

It made Byron quiver in interesting places.

"You're not wrong, friend. I'm Dean, by the way." He offered his paw.

Byron shook it gently, aware of his own cumbersome bulk. "Byron."

"So, you into the semiaquatic?" Dean practically purred the words.

"I, um... I..." Byron trailed off. There was no way he could explain his interest in this place or the patrons or how it made him feel.

How could he explain that he wasn't what people perceived? That he was a freak? That's how others had described him in the past.

Another drink arrived, and there were a few minutes of silence that Byron struggled to gauge. He felt awkward most of the time, silence or not, but was this an awkward silence?

He shifted on his chair. The scent from his new friend was stirring *it*, and Byron heaved a heavy sigh.

"Are you feeling morose too?" Dean asked with a grin.

"No, it's your scent. It's...um, unique." Byron scrunched his nose.

Dean's face dropped, and his eyebrows shot up. "Wow, you're some asshole. I'd be out the door right now if I wasn't so exhausted." The words were harsh, but his tone was calm.

This wasn't the first time Byron noticed how drained the otter looked, though this was the first time he saw it without the dim bar lighting and loneliness filling his eyes.

"You look sick. Should you be here?" Byron automatically raised his large hand to cover his mouth and nose.

The otter chuckled. "Believe me, it isn't contagious."

Byron cautiously lowered his hand and eyed Dean suspiciously. Likely, he had already been exposed if it was contagious.

"And for your fucking information—" Dean started whilst looking squarely at the drink in front of him "—I'm non-binary. Sometimes, I feel a little more feminine and wear a feminine scent to cover my musk. Are you going to be an asshole about that?"

This time the silence was definitely awkward, and it took Byron a moment to put the words together, finally saying simply, "My brother's wife is transgender."

Byron frowned as he spoke. He wasn't a total asshole—and he wasn't ignorant—but he wasn't sure how he was to know that Dean was non-binary just from the mixture of scents. "I'm no happier with other people's assumptions than you are," Byron huffed. "Which pronouns do you prefer?"

Dean cleared his throat. "They, them."

Byron gave a curt nod.

The silence resumed as they both drank, only easing a while later when the otter began occasional commentary on other patrons in the bar: their clothes, whether they'd fucked, who had topped. It was enough to have Byron squirming uncomfortably. He had nothing to interject, so he merely listened and grew more uncomfortable in his seat at the otter's words.

When they were halfway through their next drink, Dean stood to go to the bathroom and promptly collapsed against Byron.

Byron grabbed hold of the otter and tried to keep them upright, managing to spill them back onto the barstool.

"Can't hold my booze like I used to," Dean joked, but they didn't seem so drunk. More so tired and weak.

"Hey buddy, we don't want people fall-down-drunk here," the beaver grumbled over the bar. "Get your friend home, okay? No more drinks tonight." The barman walked away even as Byron tried to protest that he neither knew the otter nor where they lived.

"Take me home, my friendly bull." Dean chuckled the words out, and Byron nodded. What else was he supposed to do? He would have protested, but Dean leaned into him again, and that scent... It was *very* distracting.

Byron half-carried the otter to the nearest taxi rank, the warm salt air blowing up from the beach at least reviving them a little. But even so, Byron felt he couldn't just leave them there; he really should make sure they got home okay.

"I'm sorry. I should've realised I wasn't up to coming out tonight. I was just... I didn't want to be home alone." Dean seemed frustrated, and Byron felt like he might understand.

A taxi pulled up after a few minutes, and Byron didn't hesitate when Dean pulled him in alongside them into the back. They gave their address, a short ride away, and leaned against Byron.

"Tell me if I'm being too forward, but seeing as you're taking me home, maybe... you want to take me home?"

It took Byron a moment to understand what was being suggested. He felt a nervous sweat break out all over his body, dampening his fur as *it* stirred uncomfortably.

"That's… I…" Byron struggled to find the words, partly because he was torn in his response.

Dean chuckled at his flustering and leaned further into him, pressing their lips to Byron's with little energy behind it. It spoke of the otter's exhaustion, giving Byron further doubts. When Dean pulled back, he finally replied, "I don't think you are well enough for—"

"I was dying," Dean cut him off. "I was sick for a long time, and now they tell me I'm cured. But some days it's hard to tell the difference. It's a long recovery, and it's…" Dean trailed off momentarily before admitting, "Sometimes it's lonely."

"I get lonely too," Byron admitted.

Dean smiled and relaxed all the more against Byron's much larger frame.

Dean's loft was pleasant, if basic.

It had mod cons and amenities but felt unlived or in limbo. Like the otter was simply living there with no attachments. The opposite of Byron in many ways. Byron filled his tiny home with ephemera, remembering every lost moment with melancholic nostalgia.

Byron helped Dean to the bed and stood, unsure what to do.

"Help yourself to anything," Dean told him, waving a paw toward the kitchenette.

"I'm fine," Byron replied, shifting foot to foot and unsure what to say or do. "I haven't um… I've never…"

"Oh shit, are you a virgin?"

"No, of course not. How absurd. Do I look like a virgin?" Byron blustered automatically in response, his cheeks burning all the way up to his horns.

"You kinda do, yeah." Dean grinned.

"I am not! But even if I were, there would be no shame in it. Many people have reasons for not becoming sexually active with others…" Byron blustered with indignation.

Dean continued to grin. "*With others*, huh? You mean you're plenty sexually active with yourself? That's fine by me; I'm exhausted, so a hand job would be a perfect nightcap right now."

Dean held out their paw, and Byron found himself taking it. Maybe if he explained *it* to the otter, then—

"It's okay, Byron. You don't need to look so terrified." Dean grinned at him. "Honestly, you don't need to stay, I'll be fine."

Byron hesitated. He didn't want more ridicule and rejection, but perhaps Dean's perspective being non-binary might make them more accepting of Byron's *issues*? Of *it*?

"I…" Byron started to respond but looked down to see Dean's eyes had closed, and they were starting to snore gently. Byron stood, awkwardly unsure for a moment. Then he kicked off his shoes, stripped down to his boxers and undershirt, and climbed in next to Dean. The otter stirred a little as Byron pulled the bed sheets over them and settled back.

The next morning, Byron woke with Dean wrapped around him, the otter's paw on his crotch. When he jumped at the realisation, Dean startled awake.

"Fuck! You scared the shit out of me!" Dean chuckled and then settled back against Byron, snuggling into him. "I don't usually do sleepovers, but I can't be mad after the best sleep I've had in a while. It feels nice having a warm bulk to cuddle up to."

Byron grunted, unable to form words with the otter snuggled so close.

"A huge cock is nice, too," Dean added with another chuckle.

Byron took in a sharp breath and felt *it* react to the comment.

"Oh, come on, Byron. At least let me blow you as thanks for helping me home?"

Dean reached over, and Byron grabbed their paw. Regardless, *it* twitched in response.

"Please, don't—" Byron pleaded.

Dean's brow furrowed. "Shit, I'm sorry if I misread this. I just thought you were into it."

"I am," Byron protested, frustrated and annoyed at himself. Dean was so attractive and arousing, and the fact that they had even made it this far meant that Dean really was interested in having sex.

But that would all change once Byron proved a useless lover. Not just a lack of confidence but an actual hatred for *it*. As always, Byron would allow his lover to take the pleasure they wanted and endure as they did so. For a while, he had wondered if he was asexual, but it really wasn't that. It was… *it*!

Byron swallowed audibly and let go of Dean's paw before nodding.

With a gentle smile, Dean reached forward again and started to unbutton Byron's trousers, his fingers caressing over the downy, soft fur there.

It made Byron shudder. He wanted to enjoy the sensation but couldn't relax enough.

He closed his eyes as Dean's paw moved into his pants and slowly drew *it* out.

His cock was thick and long in a way that should be pleasing, flared slightly at the head like any other bull. But just the idea of *it* made Byron shudder. It wasn't how Byron was meant to be.

"Mm…" Dean gave an appreciative hum, and Byron opened his eyes to see their smile. Dean liked what they saw, making Byron feel worse on multiple levels.

"Nice," Dean muttered, eyes wide as they licked their lips.

"It's hideous," Byron blurted and started reaching to pull blankets up around him.

"What?" Dean looked confused but didn't stop Byron from covering up. "I feel like something is happening here that I'm not quite understanding."

Byron let out a deep sigh, a sinking feeling in his chest. He could explain, and then Dean would throw him out, or he could pretend everything was okay and have sex. Hopefully, it would at least be enjoyable for Dean.

"You're uncomfortable," Dean acknowledged. "You don't have to tell me anything, but please understand that I know what it's like not to be comfortable in your own skin, so if—"

"I'm not a bull," Byron groaned. "Well, I am a bull, mostly. I'm a freak."

Dean frowned but still appeared attentive, so Byron continued cautiously. This wasn't the first time someone had given him a chance to explain, and the reaction then was not good.

"My paternal grandfather was an Octopus, and…we were all born bulls, all the children and grandchildren. But for me, that doesn't feel right. Not totally." Byron felt the dampness of tears rolling down his cheeks and soaking into his fur.

"Hey, it's okay," Dean encouraged, placing a paw on Byron's arm and squeezing it. "And you're not a freak. Everyone is different, and it would be boring if we were all the same. Don't you think I've been called a freak in my time? I was assigned female at birth, but…that isn't who I am. I might be comfortable presenting as feminine sometimes, but I'm not feminine, not just feminine. I'm masculine, too. A large part of me is male. And that doesn't always sit easy with people. My parents could never accept it. So, if you're a freak, we're all freaks, and maybe that's just fine?"

Byron let out a sigh that had been weighing in his chest. "I don't like…*it*. *It* doesn't feel like part of me. I want to have sex, but—" He waved a dismissive hand over his crotch.

"Would you…" Dean trailed off, considering before they continued. "Have you ever tried using toys? Something that might make you feel better about yourself?"

When Byron frowned, not understanding what Dean meant, the otter stood and walked to the dresser beside the bed. They opened the bottom drawer and pulled out a storage box, which they hefted back to the bed.

"I like to play," Dean explained with a grin as he popped open the lid to reveal a treasure trove of sex toys.

Byron blinked. He'd never seen anything like it in his life. *It* had always held him back from being as adventurous with sex as he might have wished.

"Here." Dean rummaged, then pulled out a sizable toy that left Byron's mouth agape.

"W-What… How?" Byron gulped and looked at the toy offered.

It was a pink-purple colour and shaped much like a tentacle, ending in a slightly blunt end with a slit. Byron could see that it was hollow and had a hoop at the base through which to place his balls.

"It's a sheath," Dean explained. "I, um, enjoy a range of penises on my lovers."

Dean winked, and Byron swallowed again.

"Do you want to try it?" Dean asked gently.

Byron drew in a sharp breath at the thought and then nodded.

When it looked like Dean was about to help him put it on, Byron quickly snatched the toy and jumped out of bed, his hoofs thudding heavily on the wooden floor as he moved quickly to the bathroom for some privacy.

Byron took in a few shuddering breaths as he looked at himself in the full-length mirror he had discovered in the bathroom.

It was the first time he'd truly looked at himself naked like this since puberty.

His body was bulky but well-defined. And now, as he scanned down, he could see the purplish tentacle sheath that he had squeezed *it* into. And it looked right. There was a lightness in his chest that Byron had never felt before. And an ache in his crotch that he desperately wanted to sate.

It was a good size, and the sheath made him even bigger, more girth. But instead of the foreign appendage that usually rested between his thighs, he was now looking at a tentacle. The sheath was silky in texture along the topside and underneath had a scattering of soft sucker shapes. Even with his dark, furry balls nestled under it, the illusion of the sheath was all-consuming.

Byron was panting as he kicked his clothes to the corner of the bathroom floor and wrapped a towel around his waist. He felt a strange sense of anticipation that he never had before as he left the bathroom.

Dean was reclining on the bed, naked now, their fur tussled and slightly wet around their rump as they lay there, clearly fingering themself in anticipation. Dean swallowed and continued moving their fingers in and out of their ass – his clear preference – as Byron's eyes widened.

"Can… Can I see?" Dean's eagerness surprised Byron almost as much as his own eagerness to show them.

Shuddering, and with the sheath now tenting the towel as *it* became more painfully erect than Byron could ever remember, Byron nodded.

He tugged at the towel and let it fall to the ground, standing completely naked before the otter.

"Damn," Dean sighed, "you're beautiful."

They rose from the bed and closed the short distance to Byron. Byron didn't stop them this time as they reached a tentative paw to stroke over the sheath.

Byron groaned as Dean squeezed it.

"Does it feel like you now?" Dean asked, their voice husky and low, a hungry look in their eyes.

"Yes," Byron gasped out with a nod. If he could feel a little more sensation, it would be perfect, but already it felt more like himself than his own dick ever had.

Any further words lodged in his throat as he looked down at his cock in Dean's hand. It was precisely how it was meant to be, and even without the tactile sensation of it being his own flesh, it was more than he could have hoped for.

"Thank you—" Byron choked out the words, and Dean gave him a fond smile, stroking his cock gently now and using their free hand to cup Byron's cheek.

"Maybe there are loads of people with a heritage like yours that feel the same way you do, and loads of people like me enjoy playing with a wide variety of wonderful toys. Maybe this was inevitable for both of us, eventually. Or maybe it's just fate."

Byron nodded, mesmerised by the beautiful creature.

"Can you feel that?" Dean asked as they lightly ran their fingers over the top side. He could feel something, but not the caress that it was.

"A little," Byron admitted, allowing Dean to back him to the bed and push him down.

He bounced slightly and reflexively took hold of the sheath to avoid it coming off. He found it to be secure, and now, his hand finally on it, he squeezed around it himself. Byron gave a long, low moan at how it constricted around its contents.

"Fuck, that's hot," Dean muttered, moving onto the bed until their head was between Byron's thighs and sucking at the end of the sheath as the bull pumped it.

"Ohhhh" It was a shock as much as a pleasure as Dean took the very tip of the tentacle into their mouth, and Byron could feel their tongue against the slightly thinner materials there. "I… I can feel you."

"Mmmhhmmm," Dean hummed and smiled. Byron returned the smile and let his hand fall away as Dean took more of the tentacle into their mouth, their tongue pressing against the little suckers, swirling over and between them. They pulled back and tongued the little slit on the very tip of the tentacle.

Byron felt Dean's tongue hit the exposed flesh inside the slit, making *it* swell. Byron groaned and practically arched off the bed.

He collapsed back, panting and watching the tentacle pulse as *it* twitched. Byron's hands gripped the bed sheets as he tried to stop his hips from thrusting in response.

Dean drew back, sitting on their haunches and letting their hand continue to play, this time with the underside of the tentacle with fingers trailing down to Byron's heavy balls. Byron let out a sob and wept at the pleasure.

"Will you fuck me, Byron?" Dean asked, an eager glint in their eyes, even though they looked tired and worn.

Byron nodded, not just because he really wanted to have sex with the otter, but because Dean seemed to want to just as desperately.

"Take me like you mean it." Dean grinned as they moved onto the bed next to Byron, getting onto all fours and looking at Byron expectantly. "I want to feel you."

Byron blinked, his heart thundering.

His sexual experience was sparse and perfunctory. A quickie as he fucked into someone, or they rode him. Usually whilst his eyes were closed and always while he felt sick to his stomach. But this? This he wanted. He wanted Dean, and he wanted to feel the otter tighten around his tentacle cock.

Byron took a shaky breath and moved, scrambling to kneel behind the otter, tentatively placing his hands on their hips and spreading them in the soft fur there. The scent of the lube was sweet and cloying in a wonderfully fruity way.

As Byron positioned himself, his mouth watered at the sight of Dean's beautifully rounded rump. Even as he thought to reach out and touch it, the tentacle moved as *it* flexed, pressing against Dean's ass cheek.

The sight was almost enough to have him coming.

Byron imagined what it might be like for this to be real, for the suckers to try and seek out flesh beneath the fur and latch on. With a grunt at the thought, Byron toyed his thumb over Dean's slick hole before pushing it inside.

"Oh fuck, that's so good," Dean moaned. "I want you inside me."

Byron was panting and sweating as he continued to move his large digit in and out of the otter, his tentacle rubbing over their ass. He had never had much chance before to bring someone pleasure like this and had no idea how arousing it would be. But more than that, there was a layered pleasure in giving something in return to Dean.

Not that he could ever put a value on what it meant to have this tentacle rightfully between his legs. The very least he could do was fuck the otter as they requested.

No sooner had he thought how much he wanted to fuck Dean than he was removing his thumb from the Otter's ass and lining up the tentacle. He paused to get his bearings, savour it all, but then Dean pushed back a moment later, and it slid inside them as they both groaned.

"Oh… That feels so fucking good," Dean muttered.

Byron thrust slowly forward until he was buried completely inside the otter. And he could *definitely* feel that, the squeeze around the sheath. He groaned, and his eyes rolled, his fingers tightening on the fur of Dean's hips.

He could feel the otter around him like when he had jerked himself off, but so much better. Tighter. It was hard to believe from the sensation that the tentacle really wasn't part of him.

"Hard, Byron. Deep… please…"

Byron began to thrust, erratic at first, but then Dean made these sweet little grunts and short moans as he pushed hard and deep each time.

"Oh fuck… So full…" Dean panted and moaned the words.

Byron understood; he could feel it, too. So tight.

He had little experience, but it seemed something unusual and maddeningly wonderful from how the otter squirmed and pushed back on him.

"Unghhh, this is so good," Dean blurted.

Byron could feel the heat on his face as he blushed at the words but could do no more than answer with grunts and further thrusting. He moved forward instinctively and pushed the otter down further beneath him, so he was draped over their back.

Dean groaned at the change in position and went almost pliant. The otter moaned and gripped at the bed sheets, panting as the side of their face was pressed against the pillows.

"Fill me," they muttered.

Byron hunkered over the otter, fully mounting them and caging them under his larger frame as he fucked with abandon.

"Fuuuckkkkk…" A long groan came from Dean as they clawed at the bed. "Yes, there… The suckers… feel so good. Fuck!"

Byron grunted and continued to thrust as Dean moaned and writhed.

"Holy fucking shit!" Dean cried out and jolted a little. Byron went with the movement as Dean struggled to hold themself up.

Byron could feel them pulsing around the tentacle, their inner muscles gripping him. The scent of release hit his nostrils, and he knew Dean had climaxed even as the otter reached back and tried to grab Byron's thigh, urging him on to his own end.

Byron began to thrust quicker, though he could barely move within the otter. The sensation of Dean even tighter around him was heavenly.

There was a noise beneath him, and it took Byron a moment to realise that Dean was sobbing. He hesitated for a moment.

"No, keep going… Just…sensitive. Keep… Byron…" They panted and pushed back despite being completely malleable now.

Byron nodded and continued to thrust, and then Dean was crying out and cumming again with loud sobs.

Byron was losing himself to his own pleasure. He could feel everything now; all the sensations the tentacle could feel, he could. The joy he was getting from the tight heat made him almost lose his mind.

He felt it welling in the pit of his stomach, and then it happened, all of a sudden.

Byron practically roared as he came.

He had never felt such pleasure before. The tentacle pulsed and throbbed and spilled, on and on. Dean was moaning beneath him as the tentacle seemed to pump endlessly, filling the otter copiously with his seed.

They both collapsed to the bed; Dean pressed beneath Byron as he continued to spill for minutes on end. By the time he stopped, they were both exhausted.

His senses came slowly back to him, and Byron realised he must almost be crushing Dean beneath him—not that the otter had complained. Even so, he rolled to his side, taking Dean with him and caging them in his arms. He never wanted to let the otter go as he continued to twitch inside him.

"That was… Fuck…" Dean chuckled.

"Was it okay? Was it different?" Byron asked nervously.

"Different? Holy fuck, that's the first time I've ever had suction cups feel me up from the inside. I thought I was going to fucking pass out." They continued laughing, a sweet, tinkly thing that warmed Byron.

As they calmed and Byron felt himself soften within the sheath, he knew he should leave before he outstayed his welcome. But as he went to pull away, Dean grabbed hold of him tightly and shook their head.

"Stay a little longer? I don't have company often, and I think I quite like having you around."

Byron settled against the pillows, pulling Dean into his arms.

"And maybe we can do this again sometime," Dean suggested softly. "I think you're just the sort of semiaquatic lover I've been looking for."

Byron's chest felt light as he let out a soft chuckle. He wasn't sure he ever wanted to leave Dean's bed again.

THᴇ Faᴍɪʟy Secret

Aiden discovers the inspiration behind some very erotic art.

Content Notes: Trans male/cis male monster
Aquatic monster, monster anatomy, monster fucking, cephalopod sex, almost dubious consent, use of aphrodisiac, tentacles, reference to impregnation/ eggpreg, no actual impregnation or eggpreg (in this one!), squirting, come inflation.
Anatomical References: PIV penetration. Reference to top surgery scars, mention of womb. Cock, g-spot, and vague terms: sex, wet, tight, heat used for trans male genitalia.

Harrison Beck looked at the young man across the cavernous space of the exhibition room. At least twenty years younger than the regular patrons at these gallery openings, he surely had to be a student. His skin was lightly tanned, and his clothes were just an acceptable side of scruffy, which would raise a brow amongst the usual crowd.

Harrison typically made little time for students now that he was no longer a lecturer. Very few had ever piqued his interest in or out of the classroom. But this was different.

Firstly, because this was obviously not Harrison's sort of student. No, not pre-med, but perhaps an art student, which might be an exciting exploration. And secondly, he was in thoughtful study of the one piece of art Harrison might consider buying from this collection. A beautiful modern shunga by a talented Japanese artist who had a few pieces in this show. But this was, in Harrison's biased opinion, by far the best.

It showed two male youths playing in the ocean, stylised in the way of Hokusai and Utamaro, both being pleasured by the same generous cephalopod.

Most intriguing was that, like Harrison but unlike all the others that had chanced to look upon it so far, the young man didn't blush.

Succumbing to temptation, Harrison stalked, predator-like, across the room to stand behind the young man, leaning close to whisper conspiratorially.

"Beautiful, isn't it?"

The young man was startled and looked over his shoulder, taking a moment to study Harrison, which brought a smirk to Harrison's lips. He knew he owned himself well, reasonably tall, his blonde hair now a little white at the temples. His Scandinavian heritage was as apparent as the pale blue of his eyes and the lingering accent he'd never entirely lost. He found people were usually quite enamoured with him.

The young man's eyes finally met Harrison's momentarily; then, he turned back to the painting even as he spoke.

"So traditional in many ways, I don't think I've

ever seen a modern shunga quite like it. It would be hard to tell this from traditional works."

"Hmm," Harrison mused, sidestepping so that he stood next to his new acquaintance, "True, though the subjects being male is a little out of the ordinary for this theme. Albeit welcome," Harrison added the last with a chortle, and he didn't miss how the young man took a side glance at him.

He didn't say anything but didn't move to walk away, so they stood admiring the art in silence as others milled around them. When another person stepped closer to take a look, Harrison used the opportunity to move a fraction closer to the young man. This resulted in their arms brushing together, and Harrison delighted in how the stranger's jaw clenched in response.

"You strike me as too young to be a serious collector. Can I take your interest as more academic?" Harrison asked, his voice low. A rumble that he knew had a pleasing effect on people, not unaware of his charms.

Charms that appeared to be working from the way the young man cleared his throat before managing to say, "Neither. I'm an artist, and the manager invited me. We're discussing exhibiting some of my pieces in an upcoming show. And this one caught my eye."

"Well, you certainly have good taste then. I've been around this room twice, and it really is the only piece worth looking at." Harrison knew the young man was watching him, so he looked him up and down again with a suggestive grin.

When the young man didn't move away or

respond negatively, Harrison decided to push. After all, weren't artists adventurous? Open to experiencing new things?

"I have several similar pieces in the private collection at my home if you would like to view them?" Harrison took a chance and placed his hand on the small of the man's back.

The man let out a shuddering breath, leaning back into Harrison's touch, "Now?"

"No time like the present," Harrison purred.

It had been a while since an opportunity such as this had arisen for Harrison. He found himself having to conceal his eagerness at getting this man alone, in his clutches, as they left the gallery.

The drive back to Harrison's townhouse was long enough to discover the man's name – Aiden Caron – and more about his art background. He particularly enjoyed sketching bears and wildcats amongst other wild animals, Harrison discovered, which amused him—such a sweet boy to be studying predators and seeing the fierce beauty in them. And yet, he so far showed no interest in the dangers of the oceans.

When they arrived at his home, Harrison offered Aiden a drink and led him to the kitchen. He poured large glasses of wine for them both before taking Aiden through to his study.

Aiden was instantly drawn to the Utamaro that hung behind his desk.

"Is this real? An original print?" Aiden asked,

looking at Harrison keenly—without concern or caution at being alone with him.

Not as good a judge of predators, after all.

Harrison made a non-committal sound and innocently offered, "I have more Japanese art in my bedroom if you want to view them."

He kept his tone entirely professional, where earlier it had been suggestive. Aiden raised a brow and quickly lowered it on seeing Harrison's flat expression—no threat in the offer to visit the man's most private area.

"Sure," Aiden said quietly but decisively.

Harrison led the way up the stairs, slowly enough for Aiden to take in the understated but expensive decor. He enjoyed the little exclamation of surprise and awe as they entered the bedroom, passing the cabinet of fine and intricate netsuke in wood and ivory.

"My aunt, by marriage, was from Japan. She bequeathed me many items of interest," Harrison said by way of explanation. "As well as instilling a keen interest in me."

A small explanation all the same. Harrison smiled softly, remembering his aunt Yukie fondly. As fondly as she had felt about him and, Harrison was sure, about all of the Becks and their interesting family secrets. Her personal interests and proclivities ensured that she had made a good match with his uncle; that much was certain.

Harrison could only dream of being so lucky.

"Here we are," Harrison stopped before the two small, perfectly hung shunga paintings. Young men were again the subject, one pure erotica of two young men. The other had a young man being pleasured by an octopus. It was similar to many that featured female subjects – the man sprawled, practically splayed open as the beast crawled towards him and penetrated him with a sleek and seeking tentacle.

"Wow," Aiden was taken by the even more explicit nature of these prints than the one at the gallery, and this time a flush did crawl up Aiden's neck and to the peaks of his ears.

"Breathtaking, aren't they?" Harrison kept his tone low as he repositioned himself behind Aiden, his hand on the small of his back once more.

"Yeah…" Aiden breathed out the word and then bit at his lower lip.

Harrison stepped closer again, feeling Aiden tense for just a moment as he pressed his lips to the side of Aiden's neck.

"Is this alright?" Harrison asked against Aiden's warming flesh.

He felt the young man tremble, but he didn't pull away. Nodding his consent and simply remarking, "Your lips are cold."

Harrison hummed in acknowledgement and then turned Aiden gently around, cupping his stubbled jaw and bringing him into a kiss.

Aiden didn't resist, moaning into the kiss as he parted his lips for Harrison.

And then he took a shocked breath and stepped back, a hand to his mouth. Harrison smirked, enjoying the effect his tongue had on the man. It wasn't just cold. It was what one might call *slithery*. Thick and pointed, the underside covered with tiny suckers.

"That was…" Aiden tried to make sense of the sensations he'd felt.

Harrison nodded and pressed a finger to Aiden's lips.

"You seem taken with the idea of Cephalopoda," Harrison nodded towards the art. "May I be bold enough to assume that you are not uninterested…" Harrison began to undo his trousers, enjoying how Aiden's gaze hungrily fell upon him.

Oh yes, the young man had realised enough to know that something was amiss. But it was not yet a situation he cared to remove himself from.

Harrison did so enjoy a curious boy.

He pulled down his trousers and briefs to just below his crotch – just beneath the heft of his balls. Larger than most men and with an interesting texture, they clutched tight to the root of his appendage.

Harrison watched with delight as Aiden's eyes went wide. The scent of the boy's arousal was pungent, and there was no mistaking the outline of interest in his trousers. Yes, Harrison had chosen very well.

Aiden swallowed audibly as Harrison's length unfurled and swelled. The tentacle grew and surged as he revealed it. It grew to its full glory under Aiden's keen gaze and encouraging nod.

It was at least as long as his arm, tapering so that the first few inches might be no larger than an average penis. But beyond that, he grew thick and round.

"Holy fuck…" Aiden muttered, licking his lips

and tearing his attention from Harrison's cock to his face. "What are…"

Harrison smiled indulgently, "The truth behind the myths, the subject behind the art—a long kept family secret. I am as you see me. As you want me."

Aiden trembled at that, and Harrison knew he was far from wrong. Aiden's eyes fell back to his tentacle penis, hunger in his gaze.

Harrison gave a low chuckle and stepped forward, closing the space between them. He wasn't altogether surprised when Aiden's hand slid over his cock, curiously feeling between the suckers and over the thick, slick flesh with a moan.

"Would you like me inside you?" Harrison purred, "Like one of those beautiful boys? Would you like to be one of my beautiful boys?"

Aiden moaned, closing his eyes before letting out a breathless, "Yes, please."

Harrison chuckled, pleased with how responsive Aiden was already. The aphrodisiac in his saliva would have eased the way, but the boy still had to be willing and that he undoubtedly was.

Aiden stood motionless, like a statue, but for his panted breaths as Harrison slowly undressed him. He pulled the Henley off over Aiden's head, admiring the boy's athletic frame for a moment. Harrison held Aiden's gaze and undid his trousers. As he pushed trousers and underwear enough to drop the rest of the way, his tentacle curved around Aiden's thigh. He stepped closer, close enough that he could caress the crease of Aiden's ass and—

"How interesting," Harrison crooned as he slid

across unexpected wetness between his legs. "You really are the perfect boy."

"Oh god…" It was barely a whisper; let out on a shuddering breath. Harrison hummed his amusement.

The other properties of his saliva were at work now. It would be only a short time before Aiden's mind supplied a true vision of him, stripping away his human guise.

"Come…" Harrison encouraged. Aiden nodded and removed his clothes from around his ankles, shoes and socks with them until he was completely nude and trembling. Harrison led him to the bed and laid him in the billowing white quilt. Aiden's breath hitched, and Harrison knew his mind was adjusting. It was not a soft bed to him but sand; the sound of the ocean would be in his ears now.

Harrison stripped his own clothes in fluid but unhurried movements as he enjoyed watching the drug made of his body take effect. Aiden was looking around, running his hands over the bed, feeling the sand beneath his fingers.

As Harrison expected, when Aiden's eyes fell on him once more, he gasped. But there was no fear there; there never was. Between his spread legs, he could see Aiden's little cock throb with interest despite – or perhaps because of – how monstrous Harrison must now seem in his true kraken form.

Naked, he slid his hands on the bed to crawl up to Aiden. His fingers touched Aiden's feet, and the boy moaned. To Aiden, they were yet more tentacles. Harrison now utterly transformed in his mind into one of those creatures from the depth of the oceans that so fascinated the likes of Hokusai. The Kraken and other creatures, East or West, from which such ideas sprang.

Harrison travelled his fingers higher. Tentacles now wrapping around Aiden, one sliding into his mouth to a throaty moan from the boy. Others explored his soft skin and the difference in the texture of his chest scars.

He constricted them slightly, enough for Aiden to feel the press of suckers against his flesh without squeezing the life out of him. This was met by another moan and an involuntary jolt of Aiden's hips.

Harrison smiled at Aiden's increasingly hard and wet sex as he moved between his legs. He opened his mouth, Aiden looking down at him, making eye contact before he sank his beak onto Aiden's cock.

"Oh god," Aiden cried out around the tentacle in his mouth and pumped his hips up again, forcing Harrison to take him further into his cold, wet mouth.

Harrison grinned around Aiden's cock, knowing the boy felt the sharp press of the edge of his beak. He could practically hear the thundering of blood in his veins that spoke of the thrill the contact sent through the boy at the potential danger. Should Harrison snap his mouth shut...

Harrison used the moment to push the thick duvet up underneath Aiden, raising his lower half just a little, and then he moved forward. Not having to crane too much to keep Aiden in his mouth as the slick tentacle between Harrison's legs snaked up and stroked over the boy's aching sex.

He enjoyed the sensation of Aiden's moan around the appendage in his mouth as he slid inside Aiden's tight, wet heat.

It took very little to ease inside, sliding it slowly in, easing back out a little now and then before pushing forward again. The sensation of Aiden stretching around each progressively wider inch was extremely satisfying. As were the responsive little moans and the steadily increasing writhing. Harrison had rarely been with someone quite as responsive to so little stimulation. It made him curious as to how far he could push the boy. How much pleasure would it take to become torture? It was impossible to resist sliding a tentacle along the crease of his ass, too, to see the response.

Harrison smiled, hearing the sharp gasp from Aiden as his beak pressed all that harder against his sensitive flesh. He sucked down on Aiden's cock, letting it twitch on his tongue. And then he pushed further inside— as far as his tentacle could fill, all the way to the boy's womb.

Aiden arched on the bed, crying out with tortured ecstasy. He removed the tentacle from Aiden's mouth, giving him the necessary space to breathe.

Harrison stilled for a moment before thrusting his hips forward so that his rigid tentacle moved deeply inside his lover. Aiden was moaning, clutching at the sand beneath him, wincing and crying out in turns as Harrison fucked into him.

He felt for the boy's g-spot, curling against it, rotating his tentacle.

Aiden practically screamed, his hips rising from

the bed again, pushing himself deep into Harrison's mouth. Aiden sobbed and shook, squirting hot and thick into Harrison's waiting mouth.

The sound ceased, but Aiden's mouth remained open in a silent scream, and Harrison was sure it was one of the most powerful orgasms the boy had ever had.

And while there was satisfaction, Harrison had no intention of stopping.

He pulled back once he had swallowed down everything Aiden had to give him.

"Oh god… oh fuck…" Aiden muttered, shaking and looking at Harrison between his legs with apprehension and desire.

There was no scent of fear; he was too overcome to be truly scared. His curiosity and desire dampened any concerns he might have had. Aiden must know Harrison would continue to fuck him until he was sated too. That much was clear even before the boy moaned and nodded again.

"Please… please. Want you to…"

Aiden's head fell back into the pillows of sand, and his hands came up to run over the tentacles wrapped around him. They stroked over the smooth, slick flesh before gripping it tightly as Harrison's thrusts resumed. He pulled himself up over Aiden now, the weight of his bulbous cephalopod body pressing him down. Holding him in place as the tentacle slid deep, sucked on his g-spot, and curled to fill every part of him.

Aiden's eyes rolled back in his head as he took the pounding Harrison gave. His whole body trembled with overstimulation, tears leaking from his eyes as Harrison worked towards his end.

There was a strong temptation to spurt more than his seed into the boy. Pushing deeper and spilling eggs into Aiden's womb would take so little. He could force at least five in there, he was sure. The thought made him thrust harder. It had been a long while since he had considered impregnating a human.

It would be so easy to squeeze those eggs in, then fuck his come just as deep to ensure fertilisation.

Aiden was openly weeping, his sex throbbing and clenching as Harrison continued stimulating his g-spot. It only made Harrison thrust all the harder. Deeper and verging on pressing further into the boy than he could take.

He could already see the bulge of his tentacle cock under Aiden's flesh. The sudden image in his mind's eye of Aiden heavy with his brood made Harrison shudder.

When this caused Aiden to cry out and clench around him, Harrison could no longer hold back. Three more sharp, deep thrusts had him spilling inside Aiden. Enough to have fertilised a whole clutch of eggs had he gone that far. Enough that even as he drew his tentacle back, Aiden's belly remained swollen.

He withdrew slowly, his tentacle still pulsing and leaking. He moved back on the bed, enjoying the sight of the debauched young man as he pulled out, trailing thick come after him.

Aiden panted and trembled, his eyes locked on Harrison's. Defiant in their lust and expressive of the pleasure he had found in Harrison's extremes.

Harrison smirked. A charming boy with very pleasing responses. He could keep him around for a while. Perhaps he might consider breeding him after all.

Aiden woke with a start.

In a strange place, and with strange dreams still clouding his mind. He looked at the slumbering man beside him and recognised the stranger he had met the night before at the gallery opening. Harrison Beck, he recalled. From Norway, with an interest in Japanese art. Or at least in erotic art featuring sea creatures.

He looked up at the wall across from the bed, at the art he had been brought to view. It seemed so vivid and alluring, enticing Aiden to look deeper.

Instead, he looked back at Harrison. He seemed so soft and ordinary, bare as he was, with the covers pulled up to his waist.

Aiden took a quiet breath and gently pulled the covers back, not wanting to wake him. Harrison's flaccid cock lay elegantly against his thigh, quite normal. Aiden settled the covers again and closed his eyes.

It wasn't like he'd never been picked up before, and Beck's interest had been undeniable. Aiden enjoyed the man and his attentions enough to agree to go home with him, clearly not just to view his private collection. But then they kissed, and everything got trippy. He'd barely had anything to drink. Was there something in his drink? Or... was Harrison...? Was he really...? Whatever it was, he wanted more.

Aiden didn't resist the urge to slide his hand under the covers and cup Harrison's length, feeling it swell in his hand as Harrison stirred. It felt quite normal, very human. Silky soft skin, the increasingly hardening muscle beneath.

"Good morning," Harrison murmured sleepily but amused.

He slid a hand into Aiden's curls and pulled him down into a soft kiss that deepened with every heartbeat.

Aiden moaned into the kiss and heard the gentle lapping of the ocean.

Laid

Alden may have found a solution to his loneliness.

Content Notes: Trans male/male monster
Aquatic monster, monster anatomy, monster
fucking, tentacles, tentacle sex, binder, stomach
bulge, pregnancy, desire to get pregnant, mpreg,
eggpreg, graphic birth/laying.
Anatomical References: PIV penetration. Pre-
op/no top surgery, sensitive nipples. Vague terms:
wet, slick, channel, g-spot, and cock used for trans
male genitalia.

Alden dangled his feet over the decking, the warm
waters swirling around as he looked up at the night
sky and tried to forget about his shitty life. About
the once school bullies who now hounded him at his
job in the market, and just life in general in this
shitty town he'd failed to escape even once he'd hit
twenty-one.

Once the sun started to set, Alden sighed and
walked back along the jetty and towards his house.
He wasn't so lost in his thoughts that he didn't hear
the sound or notice that the gentle lapping of the
water was suddenly a churning tide. He looked
down and saw the waves that had appeared as

though a boat had sailed past, but there was nothing there. Probably a big gator, Alden figured, thinking only that perhaps he should keep his feet out of the water for a while.

The house was hot despite the open windows and the ancient ceiling fan.

Alden stripped down to his underwear, then grimaced as usual as he removed his sweaty binder before climbing between the cool sheets, happy to let sleep take him at the end of another hideous day.

He had barely started to nod off in the oppressive and swampy humidity when a noise woke him.

A thud, as though something had fallen. Alden immediately sat up, his eyes drawn to his window. It was open much wider than when he'd gone to bed, and the light breeze was moving the thin curtains.

When he heard the scurrying sound, Alden wondered if a racoon or opossum had climbed in, but then he saw it. A huge, dark shape scuttled across the room and under his bed. Not the right shape for a gator, but big all the same.

Alden's heart was thundering in his chest, and he sat frozen, not daring to move. He was trying to push himself to look under the bed and verify what he had seen, but then he heard the low, deep chuckle.

"Who's there," Alden demanded through his fear.

"Oh, we've not been formally introduced," the voice from under the bed was charming and terrifying. And, for some reason that Alden didn't want to try to unpack, titillating. "I've had many names over the years, but now I go by Brack."

Alden stuttered, unable to form words as a tentacle rose from under the bed and wrapped around his waist.

"And I know who you are, sweet boy." The tentacle did not loosen but simultaneously caressed most of Alden's body. "I always enjoy your visits to my jetty. It can be a lonely place to dwell."

"Um," Alden started, uncertain how to address the monster under his bed, "I'm sorry to hear that."

"I have considered for some time that it might be fulfilling for me and relieve some of my loneliness and boredom if I were to have children. I've just been waiting for a suitable incubator." The soft Southern drawl was so charming that it took a moment for Alden to catch the words.

"Wait? In-incubator?" Alden asked, fear now accompanied by a new kind of anxiety. He had never told anyone he wanted children; it had been hard enough to convince people that he was a man. A man that still wished to use his uterus was not something many would accept.

"A short-term arrangement, I assure you, only a day or so." As the creature spoke, it rose fully from under the bed.

Alden wondered if this might be what some would call a mermaid.

Not half-fish, but the man was clearly aquatic. His skin looked like leathery light green scales, and the long, thin tentacle and a few others of varying sizes emanated from his crotch, sprouting between his thick thighs. His hands were webbed and ended with reptile-like claws. Alden was sure his feet looked like this too, but he couldn't see that far.

"Would you be amenable?" Brack asked, and Alden had to admit he was somewhat charmed. Alden quickly shook his head, fighting the strange desire.

"What are you doing to me? Some kind of pheromones?"

Brack let out a chuckle. "Oh, sweet boy, nothing like that. I would say that there are some of your kind with a propensity to be attracted to those of mine. I knew from my attraction to you that you were one of those. And with so few of my kind, I cannot be fussy about who would incubate my young." Brack lowered himself over Alden and caressed his face, "though it is no hardship, being attracted to you."

Alden whimpered. He hadn't meant to, but the touch sent a spark through him right down to his increasingly wet sex.

He had no idea if he wanted to be an incubator for this creature; if he took the time to think about it, then he probably didn't. But he could absolutely not deny his attraction and the desire to feel the creature inside him.

"No need to fret. If you say no, I will leave."

There was a moment of silence in which Alden bit his tongue, trying not to beg the creature to stay. He was so painfully aroused; perhaps their shared loneliness gave them a connection that Alden hadn't realised he craved.

Alden didn't reply verbally. Instead, he spread his legs with a whimper.

With a hum of satisfaction, the creature moved between Alden's legs as he stroked a hand over Alden's cheek.

"So beautiful, you will be all the more so when carrying my young," Brack muttered as he slowly and gently pulled Alden's underwear down his trembling legs.

Alden shuddered, panting as he writhed under the cold scales. He was shaking with an anxious need, his stomach roiling as he ached to be filled.

"So receptive, how wonderful." The creature muttered, stroking a hand down Alden's side even as Alden felt the tentacles start roaming over him. One stroked his thigh, another curled and uncurled on his stomach. The thickest probed at Alden's sex, sliding against him and nudging his small cock.

Alden bit back a sob at the sensations, with the cold scales rough against him, warming slightly with the prolonged contact. Alden was sure no human could ever feel this good.

Alden arched and moaned when the tentacle finally slid inside him. He could feel the coolness of it slowly warming, the drag of the small suckers when it pulled out a little.

"Sweet boy," Brack muttered, peppering Alden's face and neck with gentle, nipping kisses.

Alden moaned at the way the tentacle undulated inside him.

"More," Alden muttered the plea, almost mindless in his increasing desire.

"Hmm," Brack hummed, taking Alden's mouth in a passionate kiss as he worked his tentacle deeper, pinning Alden down and moving above him.

"Oh god, oh god," Alden gasped against Brack's mouth as his pleasure mounted towards climax.

Alden cried out, his whole body shaking. His fingers dug into Brack's scales as he clutched at his arms. Brack continued to thrust harder into him.

"I will be gentle," Brack muttered as he curled his body around Alden's and went deeper. "Such a good, sweet boy," Brack praised as he stilled and shuddered.

And then Alden felt it. The first egg travelled within Brack's appendage, widening as it went, bringing Alden almost to the brink of another orgasm as it travelled through his slick channel.

Alden groaned, and his eyes rolled as his belly bulged ever so slightly. The feeling of the pressure of the egg against his bladder was strangely arousing and made him blush. The second egg did not feel as big, yet the pleasure had Alden writhing and panting. The third egg was the biggest so far. As it passed into Alden's channel, pressing against his g-spot, he came again with a scream. It went on and on in waves, more pleasure cascading as the egg continued its journey.

"You did so well," Brack murmured, stroking his rough hands over Alden's now distended belly.

Alden nodded, too exhausted to respond further. All he could register was Brack holding him, lovingly whispering praise as he stroked Alden's belly until Alden fell asleep.

He vaguely registered the muttered words, "I will be back tomorrow night, sweet boy, to collect my children. And you as well if you so wish."

Alden felt a pain across his abdomen, radiating downwards. Sharp and momentary. He had spent the whole day in bed with waves of nausea and a dull pain of stretching in his abdomen. But now the pain was sharp. It happened again and again. He could feel that he was dilating and that something was descending. He felt the uncontrollable urge to push and wasn't able to *not* do so.

Alden bore down and cried out as, suddenly, the first egg slipped from him and onto his bed with a wet thud. His legs spread wide, and he looked down to see the leathery sac, pulsing as though something inside it writhed, now at least three times the size it had been when it had been planted inside him. Before he could study it further, he was wracked with more pain, this time a bigger egg, which stretched him as he pushed.

"My sweet boy," The words were crooned against his ear. In the commotion, he hadn't heard the creature return. But now tentacles wrapped around him, and the soft lips were against his cheek.

When Alden whined, Brack stroked his hair.

"You're doing so well, sweet boy." He murmured as the second egg was birthed.

Alden was panting and crying silent tears that ran down his cheeks, overwhelmed by the experience yet not wanting it to end. Not wanting to lose Brack or their children.

"One more, my darling," Brack murmured.

Alden sobbed and shook his head, "I can't."

"You must, sweet boy," Brack said as he trailed a clawed finger down Alden's shrinking belly. Alden shuddered and understood the threat there. The egg was coming out one way or another.

"Push, darling." Brack encouraged, and Alden did. He was trembling as he felt the egg moving. Alden grunted and bore down, his scream coming out as little more than a whisper from his dry throat. The final egg was out, and Alden's body already ached with the loss of it as he collapsed back onto the bed.

Everything went black.

Alden wasn't sure how much time had passed when he awoke alone.

Alden's hands went to his belly, almost flat again now. It was strange how he had become used to being so full in such a short time. Part of him knew he should hate it, even resist it. After all, this wasn't a *real* pregnancy, those weren't *his* children, and the thing that had put them inside him was a monster. And yet...

He was immediately consumed by a fear of never seeing those children he had carried. The ones that now made his chest ache and his nipples hurt. Confirming the reason he'd never wanted top surgery, and now it had been taken from him.

Sorrow crashed over Alden; all he could think of was what it would be like to do this again. To constantly be filled by the lonely creature from the bayou that had sought him out. To keep those children and hold them close, raise them. Be accepted as their birth parent, knowing his actual reality would counter him at every turn if he tried.

Alden let out a trembling sigh as he lay in the dark, thinking of Brack and their offspring. He rubbed his belly, thinking about the future that could have been. Himself in the water with his monster and their children. No judgement, no expectations. Just companionship and a family of his own.

Alden muttered sadly, "You said you would take me with you if I wanted you to."

"And I shall if you wish it, sweet boy."

Alden gasped at the unexpected voice from beneath his bed.

Tentacles came first, pulling Brack out until he stood upright next to the bed, the dim light showing the green hue of his skin as he held three squirming creatures in the crook of his arm. He reached the other out to Alden, webbed fingers stretched and welcoming.

Alden took his hand.

ABOUT THE AUTHOR

Max Turner is a gay transgender man based in the United Kingdom. He writes speculative and science fiction, fantasy, horror, furry fiction and LGBTQ+ romance and erotica, and more often than not, combinations thereof.

For more about Max and his other publications, visit: www.maxturneruk.com

With thanks to the Kickstarter backers who helped bring this collection to life:

Charlie Foxleigh, Jacen Leonard, Dead Fishie, Skelly Boi Art, Maddy, Bona Books Ltd, Alex Blackstone, SomersSketch, Cashew Folio, Aristaello, CJ Gibson, Luke W. Henderson, Dani, Kal Clintberg, Chesh Dalman, Brooks M., Giovanni Ian Ortiz, Day, Marine L., casserole, Zasabi, August, ZB King, Travis Edmunds, Cool Evan, Snake, Ro, Atticus Thane, Ryan Vale, Iskandar Solmaz, MegaRobit, Louise Romana Wade, Booker-Garet Feniks, penwing, Justin Varney, Chris Hulbert, Nathaniel Kunitsky, Andreas L., Mnemosyne Iah Delaney, Orion Nova, Jeannie Marschall, Anton (ton-ton) Abela, Ralf Hölderle, Jo, cole, Sully Walker, Daniel Tô, Nathan Frechette, blkcowrie 🐾, Samwise Shepard, Arden, Elijah Livingston, James Labrafox, Frae Mortimer, Skye Sisk, Art N Progress, Tucker Kent, CanaWolf, Thorne, Logan Mead, Mark W., Kenneth McKenzie, Ngoc-Uyen Tran, Max, Amber Smith, Albert Lioui, You, Alexandra Fluskey, Danny, PunkARTchick "Ruthenia", Angelique Madere, Daemon Kaedes, Trae, Albert Cua, Pahn Dorian, Megapixelf, Danika, Princey, Zoey "Twigy" Lillin, and anonymous backers.